The Laws
of Loyalty

The Laws of Loyalty

T.C. Littles

www.urbanbooks.net

Urban Books, LLC
300 Farmingdale Road,NY-Route 109
Farmingdale, NY 11735

The Laws of Loyalty

ISBN 13: 978-1-64556-537-6
Ebook ISBN: 978-1-64556-538-3

First Trade Paperback Printing December 2023
Printed in the United States of America

10 9 8 7 6 5 4 3 2 1

Distributed by Kensington Publishing Corp.
Submit orders to:
Customer Service
400 Hahn Road
Westminster, MD 21157-4627
Phone: 1-800-733-3000
Fax: 1-800-659-2436

The Laws of Loyalty

by

T.C. Littles

Chapter 1

Morgan

"Okayyy, M-baby! You did your big one with this sew-in, sis. My hair is laid. Y'all hoes can keep that lace front wig shit, looking like mannequin heads with all that so-called baby hair plastered all over your faces. This right here is crisp." My client ran her fingers through the thirty inches of Brazilian hair I'd just installed and curled. Her ego was bigger than the room, and that's just how I needed it to be.

"You know I don't miss, boo." I moved around her head, snapping a few pictures of my work.

"Well, you've been missing in action since starting school. It was hard as hell getting locked in for this appointment." She took a break from complimenting me to complain.

"I know, I know. School's been taking me on a roller coaster. But you know I got you. I appreciate you still rocking with me. Make sure you tag me on your page but for Sassy & Classy."

"Oh, you know I got you—right after I finish getting cute-cute. You were smart as hell to open a one-stop shop for us ladies. Plus, the hours be banging. I love being able to pull up right before the club and know fa'sho I'ma get put together."

"Okay, now you're starting to sound like you wanna do our marketing." I listened to her spill while unplugging my flat irons and cleaning my station since she was my last client. I'd been doing weaves all day and was more than ready to get off my throbbing feet. My body wasn't used to this grind anymore. My client wasn't lying. I'd slowed down big time doing hair since school got added to my schedule, but I was still trying to fit in my day ones. Once upon a time, my clientele was my only source of income. Loyalty breeds loyalty, so I didn't wanna leave them out here cold.

"Oh, you know I'll plug you on my page, boo. Say the magic word—and I'll go live right now. You know I got them followers." Tae wasn't lying. She went viral off a video one day and has been slapping on social media ever since. It would be a major bump for my shop to get some promo on her page.

"Please," I enthusiastically jumped at the opportunity with the magic word. "Make sure you get the boutique, the glam squad, all 'dat! Your outfit is on the house for looking out." I was always down for bartering.

"Say less, boo." She pulled out the cash for her hair, then her phone, and sashayed over to the boutique side of Sassy & Classy and started doing a social media commercial.

I was hoping it would gain me a lot of followers. Though my business was doing well, it could always do better. You could never have enough customers.

I slid the cash she'd tipped me into my purse, pulling out my phone at the same time, seeing that my man had been blowing me up.

I knew he would be in his feelings over me not answering, but I was getting to the bag, which was something he knew about very well.

My baby Jayvon "Amp" Banks was one of the biggest hustlers in the dope game in Detroit. He was the reason I owned this beauty bar in the first place. It was first put together as a prop operation he and his homies were running drugs out of, but I flipped that shit and had my homegirls here working. We all specialized in something different, so we didn't step on one another's toes. Sassy & Classy was a one-stop shop for women to get a full glam along with a classy or sassy outfit that was unique, sexy, and catered to their curves. I didn't discriminate with my sizes. I serviced everybody, ensuring no diva left the door without their ego leveling up on a million. From Champagne sipping to massages, makeup, manicures, and pedicures—there wasn't a shop in the city that could compete with mine. Sassy & Classy was an experience.

Jayvon knew the streets, taught me the game, and now I applied it to the beauty business. I stayed branding and investing back into myself.

Everything in my one-stop beauty shop was tailored for advertisement. I had decals on the wall, custom hangers, and tags for all the merchandise, keychains, and tee shirts with my logo and website on them that I gave out randomly. I had access to dope money, so it was easy to break the bank and make everything beautiful and beyond. No corners were cut when it came to the contractors designing my layout, and no expense was spared when ordering my first line of products from wholesalers. I ordered from some of the most exclusive labels and designers because I didn't have a budget and ordered large quantities. I went big because I could. My name was on the deed, but the money Jayvon made off the streets kept the storefront stocked.

"Hey, bae." I was quick with it as soon as he answered.

"The fuck yo' li'l ass been up to?" His voice blared through the speakerphone.

"She up here at the shop working, Amp. Please don't come up here acting crazy with your guns blasting," my homegirl shouted out.

"I'll blow that bitch up, li'l sis. You already know," he shouted back at her. "I'on know why she playing with a nigga like I'm about to play about her. Matter of fact, see if we can get them old-ass Nextel joints so I can chirp yo' ass, bae."

"Hell to the no. We are not about to get no muthafuckin' walkie-talkie phones. You are not about to be out here coming straight through my line like the nut you are." I was happy as hell those types of phones had been discontinued. Amp would be going crazy on my line because he was reckless with his mouth on a regular.

"You know if I want it, I'ma get it. Just know it's in the works." Amp was cocky.

"Whatever, boy. Quit wasting your breath on that. What's up?" I took him off speaker.

"Nothing. Trying to see if shit was all good with you." He always kept tabs on me.

"Yup, it's smooth. I just got done doing hair. About to flame up and chill for a second before starting on my homework assignments." I pulled out my stash, already tasting the sweet buds. I didn't mix business with pleasure, so I didn't smoke while working. The worst career move a stylist can make is fuckin' up a hairdo off some high shit. I loved my brand too much for that amateur move.

"You love me?" He flipped from a thug too quickly.

So, of course, I knew some shit was up, and he was trying to butter me up for some bullshit. He wanted me to say yes to something. Amp always tries playing sweet when he wants to get over. "You know I love you, so quit wasting my time asking me setup questions and spit it out. Come on with the bullshit," I called him out.

He laughed, cold busted. "A'ight, then, do ya man a favor and pick up some money from Frog. She owes me on that package I fronted her, and before you start tripping, I already know I should've listened to you in the first place." He thought that meant he would have the last word but should've known I was still about to go off.

I was all for women's empowerment and letting a woman pick her hustle, even if that meant hustling for my nigga if she wasn't cut out for a nine-to-five, but I was tired of Amp's charity cases. Especially her funny-looking ass. Frog was a female from the hood who always had a sob story to tell. And for some reason, Amp stayed fronting her work even though she'd proven to be a fuckup. This wasn't the first time she'd fumbled the bag. But since I had to jump in the mix, it was definitely gonna be her last. I'd grown weary of hopping in gangstress mode when trying to become Detroit's glam princess. The only thing I wanted the streets to do was feed my dreams at this point.

"I told you she was gonna drop the bag, Amp. I should leave your hardheaded ass hanging for not listening to me in the first place. Now I've gotta put on my sneakers and go stump a bitch into the pavement." I was beyond aggravated. "You're rude as hell. It's always fuck my time."

"It ain't fuck ya time, bae. But I'm whooping these niggas down in Madden. If I leave now, I'ma be out of ten bands, and I know you ain't trying to hear that."

"Five Gs on a muthafuckin' football video game tournament?" I shouted at Amp in disbelief, wishing I could go through the phone and knock him upside his thick skull. "Yo' ass over there jacking off money but want me up like a runner? You're supposed to be running the trap house, not playing with them li'l niggas."

"Oh, you best believe I still got these niggas flexing that work. I ain't missing a beat. The block jumping."

"Yeah, yeah, yup. Whatever. Your story better add up when I do the books." Not only was I Amp's girlfriend, but also his accountant as well. And even though I was tired of doing it, I was cleaning money through the shop. It was only supposed to be for a limited time, but he was still dropping bags of cash off weekly for me to deposit on the bank runs. I was running out of ways to flip the books on some fraud shit, but I was making it happen. What Amp made in the streets was quadruple what the shop made, which is how I kept the boutique flooded with the best wholesale 'fits I could find. That's the only reason I wasn't pressing him to find a new pipeline. Besides, we were a team.

"Oh, it's gonna add up. I'm straight 'bout to jack this fool's money right now." He started cheering and clowning his competition for losing their bet.

Then I swore I heard his ass double up or nothing on the low. Amp was reckless as hell when it came to money. And it wasn't because he did not understand the value of it. He didn't grow up with a silver spoon in his mouth but a baby banger on his hip as a product of the streets. Jay grew up poor and struggling until he was old enough to get on the grind. The value of the almighty dollar is what drove him further and further into the dark side to stay touching an unlimited amount of cash as well.

Sliding off my custom, stoned-out crocs, I replaced them with my pair of work sneakers, a pair of raggedy Air

Ones I cleaned the shop in before and after hours. Frog was lucky it was too hot for Tims 'cause I would've slid those on. I never understood how people wore those hot-ass boots when it was hot as hell outside. Some sweaty, stankin'-ass feet wasn't sexy or cute at all.

I was pissed I couldn't puff a few times but wasn't trying to be buzzed when I hit the block. I needed to be on point for a pickup. Being in a haze could make me vulnerable to catching a fade. I hated having to collect from chicks 'cause they always came catty when it was about business. They'd be all in Amp's ear about needing to hustle for diapers, clothes for their kids, and even utility shutoff notices—knowing they were fishing for a sponsor the whole time. As carefree as Amp was with his cash, he wasn't a trick or about to donate to the cause. He'd let you work off a sac to earn your bill money. Broads be sick as hell when they done let their broke-ass nigga smoke up the work thinking Amp would take some pussy for payback.

On the one hand, I hated he dealt with bitches. But on the other hand, I was happy he made sure they knew who I was. Everyone around the way knew I was wifey, then ready to speak slick when I showed up on the back end. If it was owed to Amp, it was owed to me. We broke bread out of the same bank.

"Where are you about to go? Please tell me it's to get some food. I'm hungry as hell!" My homegirl Nakeya looked up from the stitchwork she was doing on a dress. She was one of the coldest seamstresses in the city, and even though I sold clothes in the boutique, I'd let her rent a section for her one-of-a-kind designs and do any alterations to the outfits I sold.

"I've gotta go handle some hood shit for Amp," I honestly answered.

"Aw, damn. Well, can you bring a bitch back a Coney dog and fries from the Coney Island over there? I'll call it in." Her big, greedy self actually went in her purse for the money like I was about to say yes.

"Only in your imagination will that happen. You better Door Dash or call one of your boos. I'll be back in a few, and if I'm not, put the money in the safe, and I'll see you at the party tonight." I chucked up the deuces and walked out.

Amp had drifted off our conversation and was going back and forth with his homeboy in the background about the game, plus instructing his workers on how to bag up the product after they cooked it up. It's like he'd completely forgotten we were on the phone, and that sent me drifting into my feelings. Amp stayed irritating me doing shit like that. I told one of my homegirls I'd be right back so she'd know to hold the boutique down from all angles and was in the car by the time Amp realized there was dead silence on my end.

"Morgan? Baby? Hello?" he impatiently barked into the phone, and I knew it was time to stop being petty.

"Yeah, I muted the phone until you were ready to give me your undivided attention. You know I really don't feel like coming up outta my character, so you could at least cater to a bitch." I was annoyed.

"Oh, you better believe I'm gonna cater all to that pussy tonight, my baby. As soon as I get to the crib, I'm in the guts and making sure you know just how much I appreciate you." He started spitting game, but it was putting a li'l heartbeat in my panties.

Our love story was so toxic.

Jayvon

Morgan knew I pushed pills, of course. Once upon a time, she was a nigga's lookout, bag girl, and ride partner on my hustles until I sat her down to clean the cash. But what she didn't know was that I'd gotten a new pill supplier. That was the one good thing about Morgan and that school shit. She didn't have time to breathe down my throat or watch my moves. You better believe I was dangling wit' the free time. And although I felt slightly bad for lying to her about what I was about to get into and why I couldn't catch up with Frog, this re-up mission I was on was hella important.

Miranda worked at this raggedy-ass nursing home with a large population of people with little to no medical insurance. It was in one of the worst neighborhoods on the East Side of Detroit, and most of the workers resided in that same neighborhood and worked for under-the-table wages. It was unsanitary as hell, and I was shocked the State hadn't stepped in and shut down the facility.

Anyway, the doctor who was on call and did rounds at the nursing home gave Miranda a gang of pills to pass along to me for a very nice price and the plug to a couple of his pharmacies. I was getting triple the amount of product for 30 percent less than I'd been getting with the original plug. And the blessing just kinda fell into my lap a few months ago. Per Miranda, ol' boy was hitting licks on the insurance companies by putting in claims and then having the pharmacies his friends and family owned fill the scripts.

As soon as I got near the nursing home, I sat my shooter on my lap just in case I had to blast a young, dumb nigga. This neighborhood was flooded with niggas creeping for a li'l luck up. But most times, luck wasn't shit but staying ready, and that I did.

"Yo, let's see what that mouth-work be like now, shorty. I'm in the parking lot. Come outside." I dodged a few man-sized potholes, then whipped up into one of the many empty parking spaces.

"I can't. There's no other CNA on the floor, and there has to be one at all times."

"Naw, Randa, baby. I ain't trying to hear that shit after you were just on my line running reckless. You better bring your ass out here with my work, or I'm coming up in that dungeon of death to drag you out." I was done playing cool and ready to shake shit up a bit.

"I swear I'm not playing," she yelled in a panic. "I can't leave the floor without coverage, or I could lose my job for real. I was on lunch when I called you, but now my supervisor is taking hers. She'll be back in about an hour."

"You ain't got an hour." I tucked my heater into my waistband and hopped out of my ride, scanning the parking lot. Nursing home or not, I wasn't about to get caught slipping. "What floor are you on?" I started making my way to the entrance. I wasn't but a few paces from the door since I'd parked in a handicap spot.

"Oh my God! Whoa. Quit tripping and chill out. Please don't come up in here clowning, Amp. You and I both need for me to keep my job." Her words were falling on deaf ears. The only words drumming through them were her previous threats.

"Whatever, my baby. Kill that noise. What should I tell this lady at the front desk so she can stop looking at me like she crazy?" The receptionist's face went flush.

"You are out of your rabbit-ass mind," Miranda mumbled. "Don't start no shit with her. Just tell her you're here for Miranda Curry, then hurry up here to the third floor. The elevator is to your right." She sounded more worried about the chick behind the desk than me getting off into her ass for talking slick.

After I gave ol' girl shorty's government, she slid the sign-in sheet over to me, and I penned in a fake name and kept it moving up the stairwell to the third floor. I didn't do elevators unless I absolutely had to. I had a fear of getting stuck in one, plus a nigga was claustrophobic. I was about four and hiding in the closet from the boogeyman and ended up locking myself in one night.

Valerie was passed out on the couch in a sleep coma and didn't hear my crying and banging on the door in panic mode to be let out. I was in that stuffy, too-small space for at least five hours because I remembered going in when *Married with Children* came on at midnight and getting dragged out and my ass beat when the news was on. I'd fallen asleep by then, but Valerie had woken up, throwing up all over herself and needing my help, but I was nowhere to be found. I didn't even go to school that day because of all the welts her nutzo ass left on my toddler body.

Miranda was standing in front of the elevators when I bent the corner. As mad as she'd just made me, I got stuck on how phat her booty was looking in the hot-pink scrubs she was wearing. I fucked around and had to adjust my manhood 'cause it was starting to wake up to the thought of breaking her back out real quick. The thin material barely contained the natural meat she was blessed with.

Even with the money she was touching with our hustle, it was still hard to believe she wasn't clapping them cheeks for a check anymore. Miranda used to have all the homies lined around the stage during her sets and waving her down for a lap dance. Me included. But she'd been staying out of the club since having a baby.

Randa got knocked up by this nigga who had long bread but not a lot of time left on this earth. He was murdered because niggas saw his potential in the rap game. He was about to blow up, and they were jealous of his shine. Period. The hate in Detroit was strong . . . too muthafuckin' strong, which is why I stayed strapped and ready to lay niggas down.

"What was all that stupid shit you was talking on the phone?" I walked up behind her without her ever picking up on my presence. She really needed to get a better sense of her surroundings.

She gasped, jumped back, and grabbed her chest. "Damn it, Amp! You scared me."

"Are you okay, sweetheart?" One of the residents looked up over her red-framed glasses held together by Scotch tape and questioned Miranda. She was one of many pee-soiled residents lined up in wheelchairs against the wall. Most of them was either staring off into thin air or at the television that was playing a game show, but she happened to be knitting.

"Yes, I'm fine, Ms. Joseph. I'll be right back to get you changed and to the dining room for dinner. Go ahead back to knitting your blanket." Miranda rubbed the lady's back.

"Are you sure?" The lady looked at me and then back at Miranda, holding her knitting needle like she was gonna do something.

"Yeah, she's sure, OG. You ain't gotta stroke out trying to worry about some shit that ain't got nothing to do with you. I'll have ya little diaper changer back to you in a few." I was amused at Granny's cockiness but not pleasant with her.

"You can't be this fucking crazy," Miranda mumbled, pulling me up the hallway and into an empty room by my arm. "I begged you not to come up here acting all uncivilized. The last thing I need is for somebody to be all up in my business. You know half these hoes don't like me anyway."

"You stay with some enemies. So, fuck all that. Where's my work at? And who are these niggas you wanted to throw up in my face like you'd sell them my shit?" I backed her into the corner.

"Nobody. Damn. I just said that shit so you'd hurry up. You know I hate holding." She slid the stash of pills out of her waist trainer and into my hands.

"That wasn't so hard, now was it? Next time, make the shit smooth, or I'ma use this heat on yo' ass for real." I was out just as quickly as I pulled down on shorty.

Chapter 2

Amp

Respect was something I commanded out here in these streets. You couldn't get to the top in the game I was in by playing pussy. I fucked pussy, ate my girls like a king, and even played around in the streets with pussy—but that's as far as I went. In the streets, I was a muthfuckin' monster, a savage, and to be feared. That's how I'd been keeping my position for so long. Confrontation wasn't a problem for the kid, but I was growing above it—with a trigger finger to just blast my problems and keep it moving.

My operation was getting too big for mediocre problems. And that's what my li'l homie Chris was starting to bring to the table. Whereas Frog was trying to get down for a few bucks, this nigga Chris was trying to steal the entire package and say he was robbed . . . the oldest game in the book for a dumb hustler. He should've done his research and asked the streets about me. But it was too late for that now.

The sun was just going down, and I'd just left the spot from running game with my fellas all day. Even though it pissed Morgan off that I kicked it on the block from time to time, she had to understand that I was still a street nigga to my core. It didn't matter that I was getting big bread. That meant I could cash out on whatever I wanted, floss hard on these fools, and buy the block out for my crew to set up shop on. I also owned a few properties I let some fiends rent in exchange for their first-of-the-month checks. Their houses also served as hot spots so my other customers could get high off the streets. For me, it was a win-win. And since they stayed high with a roof over their heads, it was a win for them as well. I literally sat up watching every gangster movie, documentary, and series on TV and pulled parts out of each one to build the dope operation I was running.

The block was starting to die down from activity as everybody tried to find something to get into for the night, even if that meant meeting back up on the block for a throw party. I wasn't messing with none of that. I let my workers have their fun as long as the count didn't come up short.

"Hey, Amp, I made sure a muthafucka didn't bump, touch, or brush past your whip all day." My li'l homie BJ popped up from the curb as soon as he saw me walking off the porch. He was an alert li'l dude about 10 or 11. Always on point with position and proving himself to me. I knew he looked up to me like most kids did, which is why I wasn't about to put him on the block working, even though I was a menace to society when I was his age. But not everybody had a mother like mine, who groomed them for the streets. All BJ was allowed to do was simple side errands like running to the store, grabbing food, and gigs like washing our whips. I made sure my workers knew his hands couldn't touch our weight because the young nigga could bring a lot of heat to our turf. I broke the law but didn't throw rocks at the jail.

"Smooth job as always, li'l homie." I slid a few hundred into his hand and watched his eyes light up. BJ was a good kid, and I wanted to bless him. Nothing more, nothing less.

"Good looking out, Amp, I swear. Thank you so much." He humbly shook my hand.

"It's all good. Keep that shit from you moms, though. I'm not trying to tell you not to look out for her, but look out for yourself, and don't let that shit get smoked up." I also didn't trust BJ around no work because I knew his mom was feenin' real bad for anything that could take her mind off life. My OG said she did heroin back in the day, but now her drug of choice was crack. The money BJ just slid into his pocket was the cash his moms made off their food subsidy this month.

"I'm on the bus first thing in the morning to get me some new kicks and clothes. My friends be clowning me. That's why I keep asking you to put me on."

BJ's words fell on deaf ears 'cause my eyes were busy shooting daggers into the nigga who'd been shaking me. He was coming out of this shorty's house who stayed across the street from the trap. As soon we locked eyes, you could see the tension shoot through his body. If ol' girl wasn't behind him, I'm sure his ho ass would've tried backing back up into the house.

"Yo, li'l nigga. Bring yo' sneak ass out here and face me like a man," I called him out, moving past BJ and walking toward shorty's front porch. And I dared him to shut the door 'cause I was gonna have to kick my way in. "You got my work? My money? I know you don't think I believe that bullshit story about you getting robbed, or did you?"

By this time, I was in front of her house, and he'd staggered off her porch with echoes of her door slamming behind him. Ol' girl didn't want no parts of the smoke Chris had coming his way, but if he didn't have my money, I was still going through her front door. I didn't care who my workers dicked down, but if he was slanging dick to a chick this close to where we were trapping, her crib served as his stash spot as well. I didn't even wanna tell Morgan she'd been right all along about this fool being bad for business.

"Amp, man, I-I-I did get robbed." He couldn't stop stuttering. "Dude came up from behind and put his piece to my head right when I was about to cop the work to serve."

"They took my work but left you with these Cartier frames? All your ice? Lying-ass muthafucka, do I look dumb? You out here fresh as fuck with new Air Ones on jumping off the Nike 'fit, clean cut from the barbershop, and smelling like some Baccarat. Ain't shit got robbed from you, my G. You snuck the bag and upped ya game. You did ya big one, or at least thought you did. You ain't gotta lie. Stand on ya gangsta, my G."

He didn't know how to respond.

"Oh, okay, the silence speaking loud, playboy. Is it something you want me to tell ya moms? Ya li'l one? How 'bout yo' bitch before I nut on her face?" I whipped out my gun and put it to his head. "Is this how that nigga ran up on you? Is this how his piece felt on your lopsided-ass dome?" I'd been trying to level up from killing, but the demon in me couldn't let him slide. He was too bold of a liar, straight to my face, and every bit of the liability Morgan said he'd be. He had to be the example for anybody else who was trying to plot on a come-up off my work. It was a must I took out the weakest link before the link broke on me and my team.

"Listen, Amp . . . I can work it off, plus throw you a few dollars I got put up. It ain't much, but please, let me make this shit right." His chest was rising up and down as he begged me to have mercy on him.

At first, I thought about sparing him and letting him owe me, working it off like a slave, especially since shorty was peeking through her blinds at us, but I took my gun from his head and waved it her way as a signal she'd get the next bullet if she dared to open her mouth. She and everybody else around the hood knew exactly how cold-blooded and murderous I was.

As soon as her blinds flicked closed, I let my finger pull the trigger, sending his body into the pavement and his soul to heaven or hell. It was up to God from here.

The few homies that were left dangling on the block walked off like they hadn't seen anything because they knew the street code. And with Chris sprawled out on the ground with a bullet hole in his head, the message was crystal clear—crossing me came with a death sentence. You didn't have to dedicate your life to me. You could roll with any team in the city. But trying to snake me came with deadly consequences. Loyalty went a long way with me.

"Yo, Dex, shut shit down and tell the boys some li'l nigga was trying to rob him if they come lurking. And ol' girl, make sure her loose pussy lips ass don't run that mouth as much as she lets the neighborhood hit." I snatched the Cartier glasses off Chris's face, the ice from around his neck, and the sneakers off his feet.

"I got you. And you ain't gotta worry about Vanessa. That cum-thirsty bitch will take this ice, pawn it in the morning, and be straight." I gladly handed him the ropes if that's all it took to buy her loyalty.

"BJ, you want these new kicks?" I held up the sneakers. The brand-new smell was still bumping out of them joints.

"Hell to the yeah, I do." He came running, then kicked off his scuffed-up sneakers, sliding the new Air Ones on with the quickness.

"You can have these too." I tossed him the iced-out frames as well.

"Shiiiit, this fool lucky he ain't my size 'cause I'd take the clothes off his back and leave him butt naked in the middle of this street." BJ kicked his shoes off, put on Chris's new Air Ones, and slid the Cartiers on his ashy face.

"You're wild as hell, youngin'."

"Been that way since birth, my momma said. Straight don't give a fuck about nothing."

"A'ight then, you make sure the cops don't make shit shake around here, and I'll make sure your whole wardrobe is tight for the summer," I promised him.

"Say less. It's done. You now I'm loyal to the Always Making Paper Team." At that moment, I couldn't front. Li'l homie did have heart. I still wasn't about to put him around the dope I was supplying the hood with, though. But if he stayed loyal to the team till he was able to legally hustle with the team, I'd fa'sho level him up.

"A'ight then, li'l lieutenant. I'll be seeing you around in a day or two." I decided to sweeten the deal and give him the few dollars I'd collected from Chris's pockets as well, then bounced before getting caught at the crime scene. I was sure Dex had shit sewn up.

With both Chris and Frog out of the way, it was time to go party with my crew.

Chapter 3

Morgan a.k.a. Mooka

Pulling up at the location, I got out of my mind and focused on the moment. Swooping up behind Frog's beat-up whip, I honked the horn and waved one hand out the window, signaling her to come holla at me. Even though I'd slipped into my sneakers, I was still slayed for work. I wasn't getting out in booty shorts and heels, only to hear Jay talking shit to me later on about prancing around in front of random men trying to be cute.

"If it ain't the infamous Mooka." Frog called me by my street name. Not many people knew my name was Morgan. And if they slipped up and found out, they knew not to call me that, just like they knew not to call Amp by his government name, Jayvon. "What's good wit' you? It's been a minute since I've seen you around the way." She knew this wasn't no friendly catch-up visit, so I didn't know why she was trying to play it as such.

I cut straight to the chase.

"Had you did what you needed to do, you wouldn't be seeing me now." I held out my hand. "And just 'cause I'm here now doesn't mean I wanna be or got time for it. You got the cash, right?" I was ready to collect, count it up, and bounce back to the boutique to my new life.

"Yeah, I got you." She put a few dollars in my palm, then turned on her heels and walked back to her car way too fast for my comfort.

I felt like I was gettin' played. Her whole aura was off. This bitch thought that just 'cause I was dressed to walk the runway I wasn't the same street bitch that used to sit on the block with Amp selling nick bags.

"Yo, bae. What's good?" Jay's voice cut into the speaker because he was connected to my Bluetooth.

"I swear to God you better eat my pussy so good when you get home, Amp. I'm 'bout to have to go beat the Mario coins up outta this ho's head for thinking I'm the stupid one." I put emphasis on the word "I'm" because the audacity of Frog to try me was hilarious. I might've not grown up with her like Jayvon did, but I could spot a slow one from anywhere, and she was definitely working off a pill-brain. "I told you not to give this girl no work. I told you." I peeled open the cigarette-smelling bills and counted them up to $300. She was still $200 short.

Amp was laughing. "Man, that ho got heart." He started telling his homeboys in the background how Frog was now playing me.

That only infuriated me. I was really ready to scrap at this point, swooping my long, flowing hair up into a ponytail. Even though I might've been a pretty girl nowadays, I kept a rubber band around my wrist for just in case—cases like this. I was out of the comfort of my car and tapping on ol' girl's window with quickness with the barrel of my best friend. I didn't leave home without my Nina. Her li'l chrome cold ass stayed loaded to make a bitch choke. I keep a bullet up top and ready to rip.

The look on Frog's face read she knew she'd played a li'l too much, and it was a wrap on the games now. Her expression was priceless. Hell, she probably pissed herself.

"Yup, you already know what's good. I wasn't even trying to get on tip. Roll ya window down 'cause I'm not 'bout to keep screaming."

I already had the hood's attention in my booty shorts and crop top, but even more, they knew it was about to be a show. They loved something to watch and gossip about. It helped the slow-ass day of having nothing else to do go by. I've seen plenty of scraps even happen off instigators lying so their monotonous day would be broken up at someone else's expense. The shenanigans weren't missed.

After a few seconds of stalling, Frog finally rolled down the window, trying to play all goofy.

"Damn, Mooka. My bad. I got you. That's my mistake." She started digging in her pockets.

"The only mistake you made was trying to play me stupid for a few dollars. It's the point and principle, and this point, Frog."

"Look, Mooka, I know the shit seems shady and suspect, but I swear I wasn't trying to punk you. I'm good over here, and I hope you are too." Frog tried de-escalating the situation.

Too bad it was too late for that. Tapping my foot, I was trying to catch my breath, and I hadn't even moved yet. My heart was beating just that fast. Frog was about to catch a hella fade. I was tapping my foot for two reasons—giving her time to pull off and counting down to attack. Frog mistook my quietness for weakness, like I was backing down and giving her a chance to right the wrong. She tried again to hand me the money she should've given me in the first place.

I grabbed her wrist and yanked her entire body into the door. Then I reached inside the whip and snatched Frog's ugly ass out through the window by her long weave ponytail. She shouted out for her friend, who she thought was sitting in the passenger seat, to help her, but the girl had already hopped out and was running down the street about to bend the block. Ol' girl was smart not to want a piece of me, especially because she was probably smoking my shit with Frog. Since Amp had me out of the house, I was in rare form and acting up. Anybody could get it.

Frog's body slid down the side of her car and then fell onto the pavement. That's when I started dropping haymakers on her ass. One fist blow to the face after the next, blood trickled from her nose, and her eyes were bugged out wider than they naturally were. I wasn't showing Frog an ounce of mercy as I lumped up her face.

"Yo, push record, push record! Upload this shit on Instagram," I heard people excitedly yelling out to each other in the background.

The small voice of reason in my mind kept saying, "Stop, you've got a brand to keep polished and a reputation to uphold nowadays," but I couldn't stop throwing my knuckles into her face. Back in the day, I wrestled with boys and flipped off porches like I was leaping off a rope in an actual ring. That's something else my mother hated. She couldn't stand that I was tough as nails and a bully to the bullies if need be. Wrecking Frog was nothing but a few trickles of sweat.

She was throwing up her hands, trying to block my punches and trying to deliver a few of her own, but I wasn't letting up with my swings. I was in rare form. I didn't care that people were filming me or that everyone was crowding around the fight for an up-close view. Muthafuckas need to know I was still a mighty force to be reckoned with even though I wasn't hustling with bae in the streets every day. I was in the zone . . . until I heard tires burning the pavement.

Seconds later, I heard my man. Someone shouting, "Yo-yo-yo, muthafuckas! Clear the muthafuckin' way 'fore I shoot up this shit." Amp's loud voice rang over everyone else's as he cleared a path through the crowd. "Morgan, break up off that ditzy bitch. Get up off her, bae."

"Back up off me," I yelled back at him. "Let me finish off this ho. I told you to let me sit pretty."

Jayvon grabbed my arm when I went in to punch Frog again. At this point, there wasn't even a free space on her face for a new bruise, and I absolutely was doing too much, but I was in the zone—somewhere far gone and couldn't stop.

"Get yo' hardheaded ass back in that car and to the shop right now." He twisted my arm and slightly pushed me toward my car.

On instant and by force of habit, I snatched my arm from his grip and looked up at him like he was crazy. Jay knew better than to front me off in the streets, especially when he called me to them.

"What the fuck, Mook? You heard a nigga, and I know I ain't stuttered," he responded to my glare and body language.

"Nope, you didn't. And neither will I." Reaching into my back pocket, I pulled out the few bills I had and peeled off two twenties and a ten. I had to have the last word 'cause I'm petty and bratty like that.

"This is severance pay, 'cause ya fired, bitch. Don't call my nigga for shit, with ya charity-case ass." Tossing the money onto Frog's beaten body, I had to bite my lip to keep myself from spitting on her. It wasn't that serious, but once I got turned up, it was hard to turn me down.

Amp snatched and broke a boy's phone who was filming everything, then reached for me again. I jumped back quicker than his move and threw up my hands.

"While you're around here checkin' up on me, ya better not had lost that bet, nigga. I could've stayed at the shop if you were going to speed up saving hoes. I'm out." I jumped in the car and threw it into drive, screaming for everybody to get out of the way.

I swear to God, I was sick of this street shit.

Chapter 4

Morgan

Swirling the last bit of Mimosa around in my glass, I tilted it to my lips and swallowed every last sip of the sweet elixir. The last sixty minutes of me soaking, sipping, and smoking was just what I needed after my long day. Though I was giving it to that Frog bitch like I was Superwoman on steroids earlier, I was feeling it now. Actually, my whole week had been draining, and I really needed a twenty-four-hour spoil-fest at a spa. Exhausted or not, though, I was about to get cute as fuck and hit the scene for my homegirl. Tonight's celebration was not only well deserved but also overly needed.

Finally fresh, clean, and buzzed, I got out and lathered my body with a cucumber-scented lotion, then lightly sprayed the same fragrance behind my ears, the creases of my wrists, and between my breasts. It's trifling as hell for a broad to stink, especially with so many vices sold to help her smell pleasantly sweet. Though I wasn't a girly-girl who laid on pounds of makeup, I didn't play when it came to my hygiene.

I continued dancing to the tunes Pandora was spinning, which was hit after hit of the latest R&B jams. I was vibing and in a whole mood. I was slightly irritated when my text alert went off, interrupting my dance session. It was none other than Keya telling me to get Jay's dick out of my mouth and to the club. I couldn't do shit but laugh. She stayed rude with her mouth, but it was cool. I actually couldn't wait to get to the bar and top off this weak-ass wine. Tonight was about to be lit. Not only was it Keya's brand release, but it was also a mini-concert. I knew my homegirl was extra nervous because the whole city was about to be out on some cash-out-and-stunt shit.

On the bill to do an appearance was a Detroit rapper we were all more than familiar with who'd been starting to get some play with the majors. His last song featured one of the hottest rappers out and went viral, so the guest list for tonight's party was stupid crazy. Everyone hoped to glimpse some straight-out-of-Hollywood celebrities or at least some reality TV stars. Even though Detroit had been considered a no-fly zone, many people were starting to link up and network. The common theme that everybody wanted to get to was money. All those who considered themselves hustlers, dough boys, bosses, and vets of the drug game were expected to be in the building. Well, if they got some chicken to fuck it up with.

Putting some pep in my step, I laid my outfit on the bed, then picked out an outfit for Jayvon that matched my fly. I was rocking a royal blue body con dress with matching thigh boots that tied all the way up my legs with the peek-a-boo toe, and he was going to rock a royal blue Balenciaga jogger set and some fresh kicks. Jayvon's wardrobe was hella cold and low-key. It had me thinking about carrying some men's pieces in the boutique. I could see my ladies shopping for their men—especially since most of them were using their sponsor's cash to shop anyway. I'd really been on my A-game lately when it came to thinking like a boss-ass entrepreneur.

Ding. My text notification went off.

Jos: This MF is slapping. Where are you?

She threw in the pair of eyes emoji.

Me: I'm getting dressed. OMW in a few. Is Keya on one already?

Jos: U know she on 10, boo. Hurry yo' ass up.

This time, she put a whole bunch of yelling emojis after her message. I swear Jos could have an entire conversation with nothing but emojis and gifs if she wanted to.

Me: I am. I am. See u in a minute.

I closed our chat to a message from Bryce checking back in to see if I'd submitted the assignment for our business class yet. The deadline was almost an hour away, so I thought it was sweet he was looking out to make sure I didn't miss it. I used to be an overachiever like Bryce until I fell in love with a roughneck. But nowadays, I was trying to balance two very different lifestyles. I sat down at my vanity to reply. Bryce had been looking out for me all semester, and I appreciated it since I'd been struggling to juggle school, the boutique, and the relationship he didn't even know about.

It wasn't that I was keeping Jayvon a secret, but I was keeping all the chunks of my life that involved criminal activity a secret. I even went to the extreme to drive forty-five minutes to and from school, so the likelihood of someone knowing me would be slim to none.

Me: Hey, yeah . . . I actually buckled down & submitted it earlier. Imagine that. Thx for looking out, as always.

Bryce: Wow! Look at you taking care of business. I'm proud of you. And it's all good—no thx needed. U know I got u . . .

I sent back a smiley face emoji, then opened the Pandora app to my Hip-Hop station, paired it to my Bluetooth speaker, and started putting on my makeup. Thankfully, my wand curls were finally falling right so I could start on the rest of my look. I'd gotten my eyebrows arched and some minx lashes installed at the beauty bar with Keya and Jos the other day, so all I had to do was apply a little foundation, some eyeshadow, and, of course, my gloss. I didn't have a face that required a bunch of makeup, so I never overdid it. I had a cute, chic, sexy look going on. Many people said I put them in the mind of socialite Jordyn Woods but a shorter version since I was barely five foot two.

After spraying down in my favorite perfume, I texted my dude to hurry his ass in here to get ready. Like I'd been sipping, smoking, and getting my soak on to relax, he was downstairs in his man cave relaxing in his own way. I was happy he was home and not in the streets, giving me a headache. The drama with Frog had him questioning one of his workers, Dex, and he was in a bad head space behind that. Me, however, I wasn't trying to think about anything or anyone pertaining to trapping. The fight was over, and I wasn't worried about Frog retaliating. What I was worried about was the party getting shut down before Amp and I got to make an appearance.

Stepping in front of the mirror, I stared at myself, trying to make sure my look was on point. Not even a supposed-to-be-slicked-down baby hair could be out of place, so a hater could say I was slippin'. I didn't deal with criticism well. Since I'd just gotten a whole head of wand curls over a fresh perm at the beauty shop earlier, all I needed was a few extra dabs of edge control around my edges. I'd rodded the curls up after fighting with Frog to make sure my hair bounced back. And it did. The curls flowed down my back flawlessly.

Once I applied a thick coat of tinted lip gloss and a dash of color with an eyeliner pencil, I was done. I wasn't into wearing makeup. A blemish, pimple, or battle scar didn't make me shit—especially since I was naturally pretty.

"Hey, I want shit tightened up. Whoever in the fuck owes us a dollar, I want it collected. Whoever ain't falling in line and following orders, I want 'em handled. And all the money that's been made in that muthafucka since I picked up earlier, have it bagged up and to the tee," Jayvon was barking into the phone to Dex as he entered our bedroom.

The veins in his neck and forehead were popping out, a dead giveaway that he still wasn't over the events that went down earlier. Frog trying to play Dex meant she was ultimately trying to play him. I handled Frog but didn't know his plans for the follow-through. Jayvon most often lost his cool whenever dealing with hood niggas and street business, most times transforming into a goon who'd body a muthafucka if pushed too far. Real talk, that was one of the reasons why I'd been totally sprung over him since our paths crossed in high school.

It was our ninth-grade year when I first met the inner-city bad boy. We both went to a high school for overachievers. Smart kids got in by their test scores and cumulative grade point averages while in sixth through eighth grade, whereas kids with athletic skills got pulled in by coaches. Jayvon played b-ball. Still, to this day, he has handles with a basketball and can beat a nigga up and down the court without losing his breath.

It wasn't his athletic ability that got him kicked out, but his mom pushing him into the streets to hustle. Val was a muthafucka, and is, was, and will probably die living off her son. Jayvon went from running the courts to running the streets, all so Valerie could remain seated in front of the television and do nothing with her lazy ass. The rest is history—a real deep one.

Amp was still throwing orders out to Dex. I didn't want no parts of his conversation. Anything that didn't have to do with me, my girls, or the party was irrelevant as far as I was concerned. No matter how loud he got or what vile threats he spat at him, I tuned him out and continued getting ready.

This was the first night I'd be stepping out in the streets to party in weeks, and I desperately needed it. Juggling all my responsibilities made me dull and boring. Day and night, despite the time, I was up grinding hard. Ain't shit to a sleeper but a dream, so I stayed in go-getter mode, trying to get what I had coming. I might've not made an earning the way I was raised to, but I still lived by their motto, which was "God blesses a child who has their own."

Jayvon

"So, what's the word for tonight, baby? You talking 'bout getting off with a li'l girl-on-girl action too? We can bring a baddie home from the club." Morgan wasn't bisexual but was a freak for me. We'd only had maybe three threesomes but stayed hitting titty clubs before she went back to school. I was being funny, but she went straight nutty.

"Not-the-fuck-tonight! Play with it and watch what happens. And speaking of that—fun is fun, and I know we play around, but don't mess around and lose your head tonight being friendly with them throwaways. Jos told me how you've been at the bar looking like a puppy dog who ain't got no pussy at home whenever I'm at school." She mushed me in the forehead.

"Yo, tell your friends to quit trying to start drama between you and yo' man and get a man to watch. You know I don't like that he said, she said feminine shit. And get yo' hand up outta my face. You know I don't like that shit either." I knocked her hand away, then quickly threw mine up to block her from swinging at me. Morgan was feisty when she wanted to be, plus I knew how her girls could get in her head.

"Don't put the doggish-ass shit you do on my friend, Jayvon. I'm not stupid or a fool. Soooo, like I said—don't make me put my finger back in yo' ugly-ass face." She shoved past me and started picking up the merchandise we'd knocked over.

"Are you pregnant or something? You've been acting hella bipolar with a nigga." I was side-eying her.

"Naw, I'm not pregnant, and don't jinx me." She caught even more of an attitude. "The last thing I need is a clone of your crazy ass running around."

"You think having my seed is a jinx, Morgan? Straight up? That's some fucked-up shit to say. A li'l homie I could run around and hoop with would be cool, ma." I was offended, especially since the same throwaways she spoke on was begging me to put babies in them.

"Yeah, whatever. That's what yo' ass is saying now. You're too busy babying the streets to even think about becoming a father. Let's be real. I wish I would jump to get a bump and be left trying to run a business with a baby on my hip. I'm good." Morgan always dismissed the topic of us having a kid together. After all the years of us being a couple, I thought she'd be begging me to start a family and make it official.

Although she might've been right about me loving the trap life, I was starting to take it real personal that she wasn't trying to go half on a li'l one with me. It kinda had me wondering if she'd gotten an abortion behind my back before, especially since I'd always gone raw dog and reckless up in her guts.

"Oh, before I forget, I need you to deposit this with your drop tomorrow." I dropped a sack of cash onto the bed.

She rolled her eyes and frowned. "Didn't I tell you I wasn't running trap cash through my business accounts anymore? I meant it."

"C'mon, now, Mooka. Don't start tripping and flipping the script on me again. You already know what it is, what it was, and what it's gon' be for us to stay up." I pinched the bridge of my nose to calm down. She'd been applying hella pressure on my neck to let her run the boutique straight legit, but we'd been up and down the same ropes to the point where I was burnt out. "This shit should run like clockwork by now."

I was trying to hold my temper, but I wasn't vibing with her energy. Up until three months ago, she was making deposits without any hesitations. She was even hitting me up off schedule to see if there was money to be cleaned. It was all good when she needed the money to get the store up and running.

Although I'd given her the building, it was only supposed to be a basic operating drug front, a way for me to push cash across the country to my business partner, and a way to keep Morgan out of my hair. At the same time, I handled the few business ventures I had going on behind her back. Morgan's dream to go legit didn't have nothing to do with my get-rich hustle. I was irritated as hell that she was going against our original plans.

"Look, I'm not trying to beef with you, but I don't have time for you to be flopping like a fish out of water. You know what it is. This money *has* to be deposited into your account, and it *must* be done before the bank closes tomorrow. You know what's on the floor and the deals I'm trying to lock in." I was running out of patience because she knew in full detail how smoothly shit needed to run.

Morgan pursed her lips together, nodded, then growled. "Yup, you've made yourself crystal muthafuckin' clear. Now go get your funky ass in the shower so we can bounce."

Morgan

Eight minutes later, Jayvon was out of the shower, and I was more than ready to go. I watched him rush to get dressed through the reflection of the full-length mirror. It seemed crazy, but he got sexier by the day to me. He was cut with muscles and had artwork tatted all over his body. Mad or not, my body was reacting, making me want to lick the chocolate off him. Even the scar on his cheek and the lips bitches called soup coolers was hella attractive to me. I came each and every time he sucked my clit, and just thinking about it got me horny.

By the time he was done lacing up his classic pair of Jordans and sliding on his Presidential Rolex, I knew without a doubt I was gonna be checkin' a female behind not knowing about boundaries tonight. He was rocking a Levi's 'fit, a fitted cap with a snakeskin brim, and the Figaro chain with an iced-out "AMP" pendant I'd gotten him for his birthday. If there's ever a *Paid in Full 2*, my boo could cast for Mitch.

I low-key giggled at myself, checking for him like a stalker. I was just that in love with him, though. I'd given up a lot, invested a lot, and had taken hell with Jayvon. He'd always been a thug, but I turned him into a boss. I made him think differently. I was with him in the trenches and was territorial over my man. There wasn't a female on this earth getting ready to live off the fat of the land I'd brought to harvest either. Just 'cause I'd shared a bad bitch with him every now and then during a threesome didn't mean I'd ever share all of him . . . if ya understand the difference.

After he peeped me watching him, he walked over and wrapped his arms around me from behind, kissing me sloppily on the neck. "It don't look like you're mad at me anymore. You got a nigga wanting to say fuck ya friend's party and give you some of this monster." He licked my ear.

Intoxicated with his scent, I bent over and arched my back, letting him get a feel of my thickness while nibbling on my neck. In my mind, I was saying fuck my friend's party too. Jayvon's touch always felt good and sent my mind soaring into the clouds. "I'm not," I hummed.

"C'mon, then. Lemme get a li'l bit of that pussy before we go," he started begging.

"Spread my legs and take it." I also loved it rough, and he knew that.

Not wasting any time, he hungrily grabbed me by the waist, slid my dress up, and my panties to the side. And before I knew it, he'd unbuckled his pants and had his stiff dick out of his drawers. I wasted no time bouncing my ass up and down on it, rubbing it down my slit, wetting him up real good before he plunged into me. I screamed out from needing him so badly. There was love shared between us, but this session was of us straight fuckin'. I was throwing it back on him like my life depended on it. My back and booty cheeks burned from rubbing up and down on the mirror's glass.

"Slow down that grind," he grunted, grabbing my hips and slamming himself into me aggressively till I froze, his way of controlling me.

I hissed and then quivered. His stroke momentarily took me out of commission. He hadn't given me a chance to decide to stop. After my eyes finished rolling to the back of my head, I let my head fall into his neck as he continued murdering my insides. Jayvon wasn't hung like a horse, but he worked his dick like he worked his trigger finger—back to back until I lay bodied and out of breath. I melted like butter on his dick every time, and tonight was no different. It felt like he was spelling his name off in my wetness.

"Yea, yup, lemme hear you say who you belong to." Jay was cocky, pulling my head back by a handful of curls.

"I'm yours, Amp." I was on the brink of losing complete control.

"Say it again."

"Yo—" My answer was cut short as he pushed himself up closer to my G-spot.

"What? Louder!" His ego was leading our sex session and driving me crazy at the same time.

Not responding with any words, I tightened my coochie's lips around his meat and started pulsating it to a beat within my head. Pulling my head off his neck, I wasn't about to go out without twerking it on him one good time. I like to get fucked and fuck back.

"A'ight, throw it on ya nigga," he smirked, grabbing my ass and parting it so he'd slide in deeper each time I went for it. He was on some freaky shit, tickling my booty hole at the same time, that was driving me wild.

Amp had me calling out his name and coming within seconds. He let me enjoy my moment to the fullest. When I was done quivering and about to pass out, he switched holes, putting it in my mouth. I perked right back. The mixture of my pussy juices and his precum swirled around in my mouth as I tried sucking the life out of him. I'm one of those bitches that gets turned on when sucking dick. So my pussy perked back up and started pulsating again, ready for more attention. Plus, I wasn't about to let him walk up outta here, worked up and full of cum, into a room of thirsty bitches.

The louder he grunted and commanded for me to do my thang, the harder I let him face fuck me. Then for the finale, I swallowed every drop he shot out. It is what it is. I was a straight freak for my bae. What I didn't do, I knew another woman would jump to.

Chapter 5

Jayvon

"Yo, babe, I know you ain't trying to hear this, but we've gotta swing by the trap to grab some cash and a bag of pills for you to sell tonight," I told Morgan, knowing she was about to be pissed. But the strip club was a hella pool of money to be missing out on.

"Don't play with me, Jayvon. Tonight is all about my boutique and Nakeya's clothing line—not our damn pill stash," she went off. "There's a time and place for everything. I keep trying to tell you that."

"It ain't never a bad time to make money, baby. You know that. They'll be popping them pills like candy if you're the one selling them to 'em. Be down for ya nigga like old times and take a sack in." I was trying hard to make her flip on her promise to start going legit.

"Oh, if I take a bag in, it's 'cause I'm down for us and not just you. You're not in this game alone," she corrected me with the quickness, hating for me to act like the behind-the-scenes work she did to help me wasn't enough or worthy.

"I'm gonna take that as a yes." I took the opportunity to use Morgan's words against her. When she blushed, realizing she'd walked into the trap, I leaned over and kissed her on the cheek, then ran my tongue around her ear before nibbling on her lobe. She tasted so fuckin' sweet, like strawberries and cream. "I swear I love yo' ass, girl. I'm lucky than a muthafucka to have you on my team. Don't think I don't know that."

She sighed and pushed my hand off her thigh with attitude. "Just drive, Jayvon. You're always lucky and in love when I compromise and give in."

It didn't take but a second for Morgan to settle into a mood. Shifting in her seat, she leaned against the door with a salty look and gazed out the window as I drove. I knew what she was thinking, and without a doubt, she was pissed, but we needed the cash. Her boutique hadn't come from grant or loan money but seed and stacked money from the drugs I'd slung over the years. What was mine was hers, and we had to rebuild our nest egg or at least a helluva fund for a stormy day.

Knowing what was up, I left Morgan alone. She was itching to stay calm and set it off at the same time. This act-out wasn't simply about me stopping at the trap. It was more so about the street life I lived always having precedent over things that were solely important to her. Her anger was kinda justified, but she had to give me the same slack.

Morgan and I had a long history as a couple. I hustled, and she held me down. We struggled, and she stayed by my side. I fucked up, and she forgave. As of lately, though, she'd been stepping out more and more by herself. To say I wasn't taking it well was an understatement. I was a needy type of nigga. Despite me doing my thang outside of our relationship every now and then, there wasn't a home outside of the one I shared with Morgan. If she kept hustling and hanging tight with me a little longer, I had every intention of wifing her. I was gonna have my shorty's ring finger heavy as fuck. I swear up top, I was.

It was by accident I'd met Morgan. As a li'l young nigga, I used to run around the neighborhood looking to hoop on anything close to a rim. I didn't care if it was a milk crate nailed to a tree, a recycled tire from a broke down bike, or even a muthafuckin' hula hoop. I was dunking and sending three points straight through 'em. I was still kinda sweet with the pill, but back when I was a kid, I had helluva handles and probably could've went pro with the hood on my back. I used to watch b-ball games on TV, thinking I could one day be a star.

Anyway, a recruiter from the high school Morgan and a bunch of other stuck-up kids attended was in the hood scouting for their lame sports program. They had a shitload of money coming in from bougie families with ties to politicians, city workers, and even religious folks. Still, none of that could add up to a championship win against the inner-city teams they were competing against. He needed boys with skills, not necessarily smarts, who didn't give a fuck about getting dirty for that W. I fit the criteria perfectly and went in beast mode the first day I stepped foot on their glossed-up court. It wasn't nothing like hooping into a crate or on the neighborhood school's basketball court that was nothing but concrete and rubble. I was eating up them young and privileged muthfuckas. The competition hated seeing my li'l thug team dribbling up the court.

All the fellas stayed on my jock and running up behind me, and the girls stayed crushing. Morgan was the one who caught my eye, though. She was the only one who rocked fresh-ass sneakers, was into sports for real, and didn't judge a nigga because I hailed from the city's gutter. Real talk, she upped the ante and did more than accept me. She matched me. She even exposed me to her side of the world, and not like I was a charity case.

That's why when I got on, I took care of her like only a hood nigga with money could. I stayed taking her shopping, on dates, and long walks up and down the Riverwalk. I even stayed getting hotel rooms so we could chill without my moms. I'd load us up with snacks, get a li'l weed and wine coolers, then be a gentleman until she begged me to beat up her guts. I wasn't on no pussy chase with T, so it was all up to her. I was gettin' it as a young knucklehead from one of my mama's friends, so I wasn't out here panting on coochie. I kept that part a secret from Morgan, though, of course, and let her cut into me when it was time.

Me and my homeboys always used to clown about suburban girls being straight freaks, but Morgan proved that shit to be a fact. I broke her in, but she broke me down, and I knew I wasn't letting her loose from day one. We'd been holding each other down like anchors ever since.

Morgan

I was the one responsible for masterminding our whole operation. There wasn't any order to any part of Jayvon's life before me. He and his boys, Raj and Shylo, were hustling on random corners and keeping their stashes in abandoned houses. My middle-class working parents taught me about money management and how to think critically. I wasn't raised to be a trap star. They were trying to groom me into a successful tycoon. With my background, I taught the fellas how to maneuver money, drugs, and how to tap into the pill market. If it weren't for me taking college classes, I would've never known how many people pop pills to help them stay up and going.

I didn't want to take the bag of pills into the party, but I agreed to do so anyway. Obviously, given our history, I was always down for him in one way or the other. I wasn't merely well kept by a thug like a lot of basic bitches who were arm candy. Jayvon Banks and I were in business together, even more deeply than me and my crew at Sassy & Classy were.

The lifestyle I lived with Jayvon was a far cry from the vision my parents shared for me. When they scrimped and saved for me to attend private schools, be in the best extracurricular activities, and have the dopest clothes when I finally attended public schools, I failed them horribly by running to the first thug that stroked me right. I was on the level of a preacher's daughter for how wide open I was. There wasn't enough trouble I could get into. The further they pushed me away from them for loving Jayvon, the harder I held on to him. I'd been lovin' and thuggin' with Amp since graduation night.

Miranda

"Here you go, Ms. Fran." I handed one of my patients a Dixie cup with two over-the-counter Motrin tablets in it. She was supposed to take one Norco at night for arthritis pain, but she was one of the residents Dr. Basheer was using for a come-up. He would bill the insurance company for the authentic medications but have me giving them over-the-counter generic pain pills or vitamins that we got from the Dollar Store up the street.

Ms. Fran didn't have any living family members that we knew of besides a cousin that lived down South, and she never had any kids. She was sent here from the hospital after they diagnosed her with dementia and said it was unsafe for her to live alone. It was New Light Nursing and Rehabilitation Facility that was really unsafe, though. Dr. Basheer targeted men and women like Ms. Frances—who had nobody checking on their well-being.

She was one of twenty-five in-house residents at New Light that were receiving improper medication that would, of course, worsen their health conditions and result in needing more scripts, and one of twelve patients that were receiving injections of steroids that would weaken their immune system so they could be more susceptible to developing another disease. I felt bad being a part of Dr. Basheer's scheme, but I wasn't about to pass up his opportunity to bring home an extra few grand every other week. I never really wanted to be a certified nursing assistant anyway.

I'd just busted my ass doing a double and was hella exhausted. I couldn't wait to get home, smoke a fat one, and then climb in bed with my li'l fat man. I been missing his chubby-cheeked, happy self for the whole sixteen hours I'd been here grinding. His grandmother was at my house babysitting and sent me pictures and videos all day. He reminded me so much of his father. Not a day passed that I didn't wish Omari was still living.

My baby daddy was hustling hard, trying to ink a rap contract with a major label but ended up getting murked by a nigga as they left a rap battle. He hadn't even won the competition, but niggas knew he was on his way out of the mud with a mic in his hand. In the dirty D, a muthafucka will get bodied for having potential, and that's precisely why my son wouldn't ever meet his father.

Had Omari's mother not begged me to stay in Detroit so she could have a close relationship with her grandson, I would've gotten out of this city. It's too hard for a person to have a dream in this gloomy-ass place. As soon as I stacked enough bread from this scheme I had going on with Amp and Dr. Basheer, I would make Ms. Thatcher bounce with me and Junior whether or not she liked it. I was 'bout overdue for a fresh start.

"Hey, Ma. I just punched. Do you need me to stop for anything before I get there?" I crossed my fingers that she'd say no because I was exhausted.

"Nope, we're fine. I just ordered some pizza, so you don't even have to stop to get yourself food if you haven't eaten."

"Aww, Ma. Thanks. I swear you be coming through for me. I appreciate you so much." I sincerely meant it.

"It's no problem, sweetheart. This is the least I can do to help you out. I know my son would have spoiled both you and Junior rotten." I heard the pain in her voice and got teary-eyed. I knew my grief for Omari wasn't as heavy as hers was. I wouldn't wish the pain of losing a son on anyone.

"All right, Ma—don't cry or get me to crying." I already had the sniffles. "I'll be home in a few, and maybe if you feel like it, we can watch *Golden Girls* or *227*." She had every old-school TV series on DVD that was made. I was super exhausted and ready to tap out, but I didn't want her sad and lonely.

"Oh, child, that TV will probably end up watching me. Junior has been up and on the go since you left for work," she laughed. "If it's true that kids keep you young, I'm sure I lost five years of my old age today," she cackled.

I wiped away the tear that had fallen about Omari and smiled. "Let me hurry up and get out of here so you can get some rest. I've gotta be back here first thing in the morning." I yawned, kind of regretful that I'd picked up extra shifts. But the more hours I worked, the more billable treatments Dr. Basheer got to send to the insurance company, meaning my check would be fatter on payday.

"Okay, baby. Be safe driving, and watch your back." She hated me working late hours but knew I had to do what I had to do.

"All right, Ma. I promise I will." We hung up, and I pushed for the elevator to come. I then scrolled through my phone to the music application and was about to pop my earbuds in when one of my coworkers got on, interrupting me.

"Hey, Miranda." She casually called me by name, but we weren't cool. I made it a point to keep my distance from most of these females as they were messy and only wanted to gossip the whole shift. I'd left the catty shit when I left the club scene.

Instead of greeting her, I was 'bout to bid her a farewell. I wasn't good at acting fake and friendly. "Hey. Good night," I dryly responded, popping one bud in, thinking she'd get back to her business, but she took a nose-dive into mine.

"I saw Amp up here earlier. He got a grandma on your floor?" She caught me off guard with her curiosity, but I was quick with the comeback.

"I don't know." I shrugged. "You should've asked him yourself." I looked her dead in the eyes, letting her know she wasn't about to question me, and our interaction was done. And it was a good thing she picked up on my energy because I was vibrating lower than a mutha'.

"My bad, and I will next time." She got off the elevator before I did, and I almost hit her nosy ass in the back of the head. She needed to be more worried about her funky ass smelling like a pound of fresh fish than Amp, but whatever. I was more aggravated with him because I told his ass to stay in his car. You know—no face, no case.

Tossing my bag into the backseat, I climbed into the car and hit send on my cell, calling Amp, and, as expected, his voicemail came on. We normally didn't talk unless it was about product.

"Thanks for leaving the door open for a bitch to approach me at work about you, with yo' celebrity ass. The next pickup can't be at my job because I don't want my spot blown up," I fussed, then hung up and went to start my car, but the muthafucka wouldn't start.

"Argh . . . Oh my God, you've gotta be kidding me," I shouted, trying to start it repeatedly until it clicked and screeched like I was about to flood the engine.

At this point, I was beyond frustrated and desperately ready to cuddle up in the crib. I truly hated having to hustle the way I was doing. I was tired of struggling, then putting in overtime, just to get set back off one mishap. If Omari were here, I'd be doing nothing but raising our son. A chick needed a break from being a grown-up.

After calling Omari's mom with the current events and change of plans, I busied myself on Google to see what was wrong and if it was a quick fix. I was trying to stack my money, not spend it on incidentals, but it always seemed like some random-ass expense was popping up from nowhere. It was always something. And today's trouble could've been anything from the radiator to the transmission to the starter. Who knew that when Sav called himself giving me that "pain and suffering" cash, he was burning bread on a bitch. That's the money I was about to spend on the tow truck.

"My bad, Shari. I hate that I even had to call you." I got into the passenger seat of my homegirl's car.

"It's all good. I know how shit be." She passed me the blunt she was puffing on. "You wanna hit this to settle your nerves while we wait on the tow truck?"

"Hell yeah. Thank you." I took the blunt and started puffing on it like I'd never had weed before. "Damn, Shari . . . Where'd you get this shit from? It's hittin' super hard." I'd been stuck getting basic bags of Kush from the boy who lived near me because he'd always drop them off whenever.

"Bop. His set is the only one in the city that's slanging eighths for twenty-five, and the shit be hitting."

"Twenty-five? Straight up? That's live as hell."

"How you ain't know that, sis? You ain't fucking around with Amp no more? Bop works for his set." Shari's bluntness didn't catch me off guard. She'd always been the "I say what's on my mind" type of person, but it was never done maliciously where I took it as digs.

"Naw, not like that. But me and him weren't ever on no kicking it shit. All we did was trick. I threw my ass, and he threw his cash."

"Hm. Oh, okay. I could've sworn . . . but that ain't my business." She zipped her lips and threw away the key like we were in kindergarten. Then she changed the subject. "So, what's up with li'l man? I see all the pictures you be posting on the Gram, but my nails be too long to tap and like 'em." She waved her hot-pink claws around so I could see she wasn't lying. "He's cute as hell, but not enough to make a bitch have baby fever." She burst out laughing.

"Thank you for making me laugh. But he's doing good, just growing. I miss a lot of time with him because I'm always at work."

"Ugh, girl . . . Why are you working anyway? I mean, I understood why you sat down from stripping while you were pregnant and big O, but what's your rationale behind working fifteen-hour shifts for less than fifteen dollars an hour . . . when you could make five hundred in less than five hours on your worst day? Make it make sense, sis." Shari was being brutally blunt again.

"Wow, you really just shitted on me, didn't you? I should've just called a Lyft."

"But you couldn't because you spent all your spare cash on a tow truck, which further proves why you should just ride to the spiz—not with me, and do at least one set. Them niggas will be so thirsty to tip yo' ass since you've been off stage for so long that you'll have me taking you to the dealership in the morning for a new ma'fuckin' whip." Shari was geeking up my head.

I'd stopped stripping in the first place because my baby daddy wanted me out of the club. He used to rag on me heavy because he hated that his fellas had seen me naked. He hated that shit with a passion, but he loved me too much to let that interfere with our relationship. We were building something real.

But now, the only thing real was my bills and the tow truck driver saying my car's radiator had gone bad and the repair could be upward of $400 or more. Shit was all bad. Rent and bills were due. I had to get Pampers and shit, plus Omari's mom needed a few dollars for Bingo and her day-to-day essentials. I wasn't trying to dip into my getaway stash, but the more I ran back my responsibilities, the more backed into the corner I felt. Or should I slide back up the pole?

"So, what's up, girly? I see you over there thinking. Are you in your feelings and mad at a bitch because I came at you? Or are you like, hell yeah, I'm 'bout to rock that stage?"

"As bad as I wanna tell you to drop me off at the crib, the money is calling me."

"Hell yeah, Molly, baby! Answer that bitch. Let's get this bread." She called me by my dancing name because my twerking used to have niggas like they were on drugs.

Chapter 6

Jayvon

Recklessly, I ran stop signs and traffic lights as I coasted toward my spot. Dex already had my money bagged and ready, so I wasn't expecting any delays or slow-ups. As soon as I parked the car, Morgan moved to get out.

"Naw, yo' ass is good in that seat." I was firm, throwing my hand over her chest, holding her still. "You've got me fucked up if you think I'm about to let you parade all that ass you've got poppin' out of that tight dress in front of these gritty-ass bums. You're lucky I ain't nut up on ya ass earlier for fighting Frog in those little bitty-ass shorts. Fall back, and I'll be out in a second."

She smacked her lips and pushed my arm away. "Make it a *split* second, Jayvon. A split fuckin' second. I don't want anyone getting the wrong idea, thinking I'm the trap house poster child or whatever."

"Ha-ha, a trap house poster child? Naw, babe. Everyone knows you're the wifey of a trap house poster child, with ya reptilian fighting ass," I joked about her knuckling up with Frog again. She laughed in the middle of rolling her eyes.

Kissing her lips, I ran my hand up her thigh and tapped her twat before climbing out of the car. I loved getting a rise out of Morgan. When I looked back, I saw her eyes squinted with her lips pursed in pleasure. She couldn't fuss at a nigga if she wanted to.

"*Whooty-hoo.*" I made a special call out to the fellas on the block who were hustling underneath me. "Get to work, muthafuckas." They weren't looking like they were making money; more like wasting mine. Dex was gonna have to tighten up his crew since he was in charge of running the trap for me. I'd had my foot on this nigga's neck all day.

"Yo, Dex, meeting time," I called into the house when I hit the door. "Did you holla at that cat, or do I need to pay his baby moms a visit?" Right off the rip, I wanted my money. I ain't had no kids, so I wasn't about playin' no games. I wanted to know where the li'l nigga was who owed me for some work—and I wasn't above busting bullets over a few dollars. What's mine was precisely that—muthafuckin' mine. Morgan hadn't gotten her quick temper from her upbringing but from being around me.

Dex threw up his hands like I was the police. "Dawg, chill. I got at that nigga, and he wasn't doing shit but running his mouth like a bitch apologizing. So, I'ma make up for the loss out of my own pocket. Plus, I told li'l fella to go roll with another set 'cause that bullshit he tryin' to run is straight unacceptable." Stumbling over his words, Dex was trying to inform me on how he'd addressed the situation he'd called me on earlier.

"Naw, that ain't good enough. If he couldn't roll right for me, li'l fella ain't gonna grow no balls with another set and roll against me. Dead his ass, either you or someone you send." I put the command onto the floor, expecting it to be carried out.

"Done." Dex agreed to it without hesitation.

"Good."

"But on the money tip, boss, let a nigga make it right." Digging into his pocket, he peeled off the money the young boy brought to me for the work jacked off.

Instead of the boy coming back with my return on the pills he got fronted, he'd returned with a mouthful of excuses and pleas for more time. Though Dex sent him away with a sound mind, I wanted that mind of his splattered all over the pavement for him trying to play me. And whoever knew . . . would know. You don't get street credentials and to the level of being a boss by playing pussy.

"We good?" Dex asked as he handed over the bills.

Taking the money, I nodded and shook his hand. "I can respect a man who rights his wrongs. We better than good as long as you stay doing right by me and taking care of shit around here in my absence."

Dex was a worker I considered beneath me but definitely worthy of my respect. He was fresh in the game but had muscle like a muthafucka. I wasn't juicing up his ego because he'd handed me a few dollars. He really did hold it down heavy in my absence. As shit continued to change in the game involving Morgan and me, I was sure his importance around here would grow. That's why I needed him to tighten up.

It ain't many women out here that'd trade their silver spoon for a chrome-plated pistol, but Morgan had, which made her rare. As of now, she, me, my cousin Shylo, and my ace Raj ran a four-way-split drug ring. We had a trap house that Morgan and I oversaw, while Shylo and Raj pushed weight up the highways.

Every other day, the two of them hit the road driving two separate vehicles en route toward Pennsylvania, delivering dope and pills in exchange for cash. We had the game sewn up as a team, but that didn't mean I wasn't hungrier for more. I didn't get into the dope game to retire. I saw myself being a true OG of the game. The plug. The supplier.

Dex kicked it to me about a few additional things going down I needed to know about while I collected a Ziplock bag of pills and eyeballed the money in the duffel bag. Getting ready to fall back for a few minutes more to tell Dex how to handle the minor situations, I looked through the missing slot of the window blind, my intuition telling me something was up. I was glad I had. My instincts were usually on point.

"Yo, you know somebody whippin' a rusty black Lincoln?" I questioned Dex, reaching for my heater.

"Naw, nope," he answered, shaking his head while pulling his pistol from underneath his shirt. "But I'm right by ya side to find out."

Swinging the door open, Dex and I stepped onto the porch with our weapons aimed.

"Yo, blood, get up out of my woman's face and see me." I was like a monster when it came to protecting what was mine.

Chapter 7

Morgan

It all happened so fast . . .

Putting my phone back into my purse from texting Nakeya that I was on my way, I looked up to headlights coming up the street, blinding me. Their high beams were on. Throwing my hand up to block the intensity of the glare, I peeked between them to watch the car. You can never be too careful when hustling in the streets, especially when you've just been in a fistfight earlier. I didn't think Frog would come back lookin' to get at me, but I braced myself for war simply because I know how Karma can come when you least or don't expect it.

Slowly driving up the block, seeming suspect, the car stood out because this deserted-ass block didn't house families, only broken homes with fiends as the head honchos in charge instead.

My gut was telling me something bad was up. When the unfamiliar Lincoln stopped right beside me and started rolling down the window, I dropped my hand and grabbed my gun. This was the second time I'd had my Nina out to do damage in less than twelve hours. They might've gotten the first one sprayed, but they fa' damn sho wasn't about to have the only ones in the air. I never left home without my pretty pistol.

"Hey, sweetheart, can you roll your window down some more?" a man shouted to me from the car.

"Naw, she can't roll her window down, son. Who are you, and whatcha' want with my lady? And I suggest ya get ta talking fast." Jayvon emerged out of the house, calling ol' boy to answer quickly. He was accompanied by Dex, who also had his pistol ready to fire.

That was one thing about Jayvon Banks—he never rode like a ho, him or the niggas that worked for him. Not knowing if I was about to be a part of a shootout, I slid down in my seat, about to crack the car door to jump out, but kept my pistol aimed toward the suspicious car.

If only we would've taken our ass to the club . . . I wasn't a punk, but the thought still crossed my mind.

"Hey, yo, bro. You're just the man I was looking for. It's me, Jinx," the man shouted out of the car, then climbed out with his hands held up. "It's fam, dog. Don't shoot."

Right as I was getting ready to let 'er rip, Jayvon spoke up and spoke back, seeming like he was looking at a ghost. I piped down real quick to see who the stranger was. Loosening my grip on my piece, I slid up quickly and rolled the window down all the way to hear every word. This wasn't a drive-by but a reunion.

"Get the fuck outta here! I must be high as fuck to be seeing yo' nutty ass, nigga. I thought they buried yo' ass underneath the jail." Lowering his gun, Jayvon signaled to his workers to lower their weapons too.

By now, almost every dude on the block had drawn their weapons, and Jayvon met up with the random man I'd never heard of or seen before in the front yard, which was actually more like patches of dirt, weed, and dandelions.

"What's the word, bro?"

Bro? Is he serious? I was thrown off by Jayvon's salutation to ol' boy. Since when did his ass play friendly to niggas? In all the years of us kicking it and being together, I ain't never known for his momma to have another kid or for him to know his father to know if he did have siblings. I really wanted to know how Jayvon and Jinx were linked to each other 'cause, as true family, they were not.

"Ain't nothing popping off. Unfortunately, the few connects I thought I'd made in prison didn't pan out to nothing but dead-end missions and dry runs. It wasn't shit but jail talk 'cause they ain't have shit else better to do. Ya feel me?"

I smacked my lips, already knowing what this random pop-up was about. It didn't take a genius to read between the lines. Jailbird Jinx was thirsty and trying to get on through Jayvon with some work. However, with me having somewhere to be and our circle already being tight, his begging or Jayvon's pity party session wasn't about to go down on my watch. I didn't know who Jinx was and couldn't care less about his struggle story. What I *did* care about was Nakeya's brand release party.

Distracted from their conversation, whoever rode with this Jinx character moved and caught my attention. When I turned to return the stare, he ducked back, tilted the brim of his hat farther down, and looked the other way. In our environment, that type of body language meant you were on some shady shit. I was over being patient at that very moment.

"Um, excuse me . . . but, Jayvon, did you forget it was my night, and we have somewhere to be?"

Both their heads spun my way, but Jinx responded first.

"Oh shit! Say it ain't so. My nigga done grown up and got him a li'l firecracker, huh? Chill out, shawty. You can have yo' manz back in a second," he cut into me nonchalantly, like I was some type of basic broad.

Swinging the car door open, I stepped out like a lady with the sole intention of putting him in his place like a bitch. If I *was* a firecracker, he'd lit the wick, and it was on. I didn't care who he was to my man. He wasn't shit to me. "Um, Jinx . . . I know you don't know me, so let me introduce myself. My name is Morgan, I'm Jayvon's woman, and I ain't got no chill. I was talking to my nigga—*not* you." Done checking him, I turned to Jayvon with my face red and ripped. "Now, Jayvon, you already know what tonight is. Can you come on?"

While Jayvon was busy looking embarrassed and shocked that I'd put him on blast, Jinx looked at me like he wanted to put his fist through my face. I didn't care, though. Well, I cared but wasn't worried. Jinx was dead wrong for addressing me in the first place. He and Jayvon had a history, *not* he and I. And from how our first interaction was going down, I'd be cool not seeing him ever again in life. If I'd cut my parents off, I'd surely cut a stranger off. Fuck Jinx and the random man who drove him here in the Lincoln. Jayvon finally cleared his throat, then responded.

"A'ight, bro. You got my cell, so hit me up when you trying to get put on with something. I got you fa'sho, but me and shawty got moves to make right now. Matter of fact, if you ain't got shit up, swing through the titty bar and come live it up with me and my crew. We'll be there celebrating my girl's boutique and shit, so all drinks and smoke is on me."

Simultaneously, my lips twisted in repulsion as my hands flew to my hips. I was pissed at Jayvon's open invitation to a party that wasn't his. I didn't care how much he had invested in me. As far as I was concerned, Jinx was a jerk and not welcomed in my presence ever again.

Jinx noticed my reaction, smirked, and then responded like he was intentionally trying to get underneath my skin. "Yeah, me and my goonies might slide through that joint. I been wanting to slap some asses and suck on some titties since I walked up outta tha pokey." He was being disrespectful on purpose.

I was seething.

"Yo, bro, history or not, fall back with all that quick-lip shit with my girl. I ain't cool with it, so make that my last time putting that in the air to you."

"Aw, naw, bro, we good. No need to go Rambo on a ma'fucka." Jinx copped out, throwing his hands up, taking two steps back. "I'll let you and your firecracker keep it moving, and I'll hit you up when I've got that bread to get on. Thanks for the invitation, but no thanks." He was talking to Jayvon, but his beady eyes shifted to me.

Wanting to jump up and down screaming that I was a bad bitch, I slid back into the car and shut the door. What was known didn't need to be said.

"A'ight, we good. Hit me up so you can get off craps." Jayvon shot him a sneak diss.

The two of them said their goodbyes, and then Jinx climbed back into the car, getting driven off by the guarded driver I'd never got to see but a shadow of. I was on Jayvon's head before they reached the end of the block.

"So, since when do you let random niggas address me? Who in the fuck is Jinx? Why are you giving him passes and shit?" Sitting up in my seat, I kept pointing my finger back and forth in his face. "I swear to God that nigga should've never been able to say one word to me!" I was going wild. I hated being disrespected. "That's the second time today. Don't let there be a third."

Reaching over, he put his hand between my legs, grabbed my neck, and yoked me up like a cat. "Calm. The. Hell. Down. Now." I was turned up and mad at him at the same time. As soon as I stopped shifting in my seat, he released his grip on my neck but tightened it on my thigh. "Don't ever question if I'm gonna protect you or not. You know damn well I'm not letting you get touched. As far as Jinx goes, let that nigga fall off yo' mind, and we'll talk about him tomorrow."

Chapter 8

Morgan

We were over an hour late, but I wasn't about to let our tardiness ruin the whole night. All I needed was a few shots in my system to perk me up again. The club was swarming with supporters for Keya. The city had really shown up and out for my girl, but I hadn't expected anything less. She'd been humbly hustling with intent for years with some of the hottest names in the city, so her fan base was popping and through the roof. This brand release party was doing numbers.

Amp was close on my backside as we navigated through the crowd toward all the pink and gold metallic balloons that lined the archways around VIP. He kept grabbing my booty whenever we were in gridlock, always on some frisky shit, but I was all in and living in the moment. It felt good being out with my man. I couldn't even front. School had turned me a little boring because I was always studying or trying to get my rest up. I was about to push everything about a responsibility to the back of my mind tonight, though—and get lit how we used to.

Keya spotted us before we got to her VIP section and started calling me out. "It's 'bout time you showed up." She was in full party mode with a Champagne bottle in one hand and a blunt in the other. Jos wasn't lying.

"Congratulations, Keya, pooh. I'm so proud of you." I embraced my friend and gave her a big bear hug until we both toppled over. "You deserve all this praise and more. You've been busting yo' butt day in and out, and now it's your time to shine." I was truly happy for her come-up. And not just because her success meant more success for me. There was enough money out there for all of us to eat.

"Oh my God . . . . Thank you, frienddd! Please don't make me cry again. You know I've been waiting on this day for forever." She was grinning and glowing like she should have been. "Heyyy, bro. I see you back there hiding and shit. Don't be scurrred, though. I'm not about to curse you out for making my boo tardy to my party." She looked around me to where Amp had sat down and started rolling up.

"Yo' drunk ass is crazy as hell, sis. I'on even know if I should buy you a congratulatory bottle or an ice-cold bottle of water." He waved one of the two waitresses assigned to Keya's section our way.

"Don't play, bro. I bet not catch nobody over here with a water." She spun around in a circle, pointing her finger at everybody in her section.

"Yup, yo' ass is lit." Amp licked the blunt and sparked it up. "This is 'bout to be an interesting night, fa'sho. I can't wait till my fellas get here." I already knew he, Shylo, and Raj were gonna show out, especially when Barz hit the stage. He was on the ticket tonight to perform. I knew every word of every track that nigga made because Amp stayed bumping his music. Everybody on the East was fucking with Barz hard because they all grew up with him.

The waitress came over and took Amp's order: a bottle of 1738, a bottle of Cîroc, and two bottles of Champagne. He was laying the spread out for when Raj and Shylo arrived. Ain't no telling how much money we were about to blow tonight once it was all said and done.

"Tell this lady what you drinking on, wife," Amp started peeling some bills out of his wad of cash to pay her.

"Bring me some Crown Royal Apple, cranberry juice, and a Red Bull." I knew I could handle dark liquor better than light. Not only would I be on one of these poles like I was chasing a check off some light liquor, but I also wouldn't make it to school in the morning because my head would be in a bucket full of vomit. I'd never been able to handle my high when I was buzzing off tequila, vodka, and even some Moscato if I'd had enough glasses of it.

"Damnnn, diva, I see you out here shining. Ay, yo, DJ, play 'Ice Me Out.'" Jos came up on the mic, hyping me up about my A Unique Piece pendant. "This bitch is niceeee, sis." She got a closer look at it.

"Thanks, boo." I started dancing to the beat of the song as it began to bump through the club. Jos was hosting the event, so she and the DJ were synced up. He even shined the spotlight on our section so we could rev it up with our Rolex watches in the air.

"You got it jumping in here, Jos. I done broke a sweat, and it ain't been five minutes."

"I don't even be trying." She blushed and batted her long eyelashes sweetly. "But let's take some pictures and go live real quick. One of the bouncers said we're filled to capacity with a line still waiting to come in. I wanna stunt that I'm hosting a sold-out event." Jos lived her life for social media.

Amp was our photographer until his fellas Raj and Shylo showed up. His three plus my three made us a force to be reckoned with, plus personal security for me and my girls. I wasn't counting none of the other stragglers who'd come with Keya. Her friends weren't my friends. I don't care what you think; that shit ain't gotta be like that.

The DJ shouted out our section, prompting us to take shots and cheers to celebrate Nakeya's success. After soaking it up, she was ready to work off some of her buzz dancing. Since she worked in the locker room of strip clubs, she learned all the hottest dance moves when the girls practiced in the locker room, then performed on stage. Her bank would've been major if she had been a stripper. She told me and Jos to keep up, leading us to the dance floor with her hand in the air, moving to the beat.

Every part of her body vibrated in sync with the music, making her look flawless. I was kinda jealous of how sexy she looked while getting down. Her hair was flowing each time she popped. I couldn't stop staring at her booty. Back when I first met Nakeya in the club, I didn't bring her around Jayvon because she was too sexual and seductive. I wasn't worried nowadays, however. I'd given Jayvon the opportunity to hit us both simultaneously, and he turned it down. That meant he wasn't trying to fuck, so I could trust her. She'd been my girl, and I'd been cool with her hanging around him ever since.

Both Jocelyn and I followed her lead and got a routine going pretty quickly. It was all in fun for us. Nakeya needed to unwind because she was always sewing and customizing, and I needed a diversion from my hectic life. Jos, however, didn't have a pastime and was looking for trouble. Out of the three of us, she was the youngest and had little to lose. That meant she was often popping off first and thinking later, which included thanking me and Keya for beating the brakes off a bitch on her behalf.

Dancing and snapping pics, my girls and I were having a ball. My whole team was lit. Whether it was drugs or legal money, we'd all worked hard to live within the celebration going on around us while making our own party at the same time. There might've been a room full of ballers and bad bitches, but wasn't none of them fuckin' with us. Bottle after bottle, blunt after blunt, and shot after shot, I couldn't believe I hadn't fallen to the ground. Barz, the rapper, and his entourage were even partying with us. Life felt good sitting at the top.

I went live with Jos's phone so she could entertain her followers. She had over a thousand viewers and wasn't doing shit but singing, blowing out hookah smoke, and showing different angles of her body. Now and then, she'd shout, "Keya, Sassy & Classy," and the venue—but my girl was in her zone and feeling herself to the max. I couldn't blame her, though. I saw the comments and her DM jumping with niggas who wanted to Cash App her money just so their timelines could stay looking pretty. I low-key wondered if my girl was trickin' on the web, sending naked pictures and shit.

"What you drinking on? You wanna taste a li'l bit of this Jossy-Baby Jungle Juice?" She swirled her cup around in my face. "My girl Nita is the bartender tonight, and she made me my own special pitcher."

"Uuum, sure. Why not?" I knew I was risking it all with school in the morning but was feeling the need to let go and live.

"Cheers." She tilted the cup back in my mouth. "Nita ain't light-handing none of the drinks coming to this section. We're all about to be fucked up. Period!"

Right on time, the waitress returned with our bottles, and from there, it got lit. Me, Amp, and Jos took a few shots as a trio. Then Raj and Shylo showed up already on ten and didn't waste time calling some girls over to trick some cash off with. It was a good thing I wasn't insecure because they were bustin' it wide open for Jayvon too. Money was flying everywhere.

"Oh, okay. I see what time it is up in this muthafucka. Moneyyyy time! All I wanna see is green on the floor and in the air. All the broke, red-flag niggas be quietttt!" Jos got on the mic and started hyping up the dancers so they could run up a check. She'd gotten so laid-back with the crew that I'd forgotten she was working.

"Ay, yo, li'l Nina Brown. I got a few dollars for you to twerk that fatty up on me." Jayvon waved me over with a devilish grin on his face.

"Oh, naw, playboy. I'on want your few dollars. I'll take the whole sac." I cupped his dick print and jiggled his balls through his joggers.

"Aah, that's what we doing?" He pulled me down on his now stiff dick, and I started doing my thang like I was busting it down for a buck. At least fifty pretty dancers were in here, but he was checking for my attention. I'd be damned if I wasn't about to give it to him.

Jos must've peeped me in action and told the DJ to play my ratchet girl song 'cause Meg's song "Body" rang through the club, and I started bouncing my booty till my thighs ached. I'd even stood up on the bench and was throwing it in his face. Jossy's Jungle Juice must've had something else off in it 'cause I was hella lit and couldn't come down off the high.

"Gotdamn, girl. Fuck your friend and her fashion show. Let's bounce." Amp grabbed and pulled me down onto his lap and nestled his face into my chest like a baby.

"I can'ttt," I whined, "but you better believe I'm going to run all that back on you in bed when we get home."

"Oh yeah, I'ma make sure your drunk ass don't pass out first," he laughed. Then we started dancing to the R&B mix the DJ flipped to. It felt so good lying against his chest and being chill for a second. I tuned out everything and took in the moment as he held me close like it was just the two of us in the room. I loved Amp so much, and I swore I felt his heart beating inside of my own chest. But something told me this was the calm before the storm, though . . .

Jos parted ways with the crew for a while, doing her hosting thang. Over the microphone, she was shouting out people and stirring up everyone's adrenaline before Barz hit the stage. He would rap a few tracks before Nakeya's fashion show, which she'd excused herself from the VIP section to prepare for.

With my girls handling their business, I was laid-back in the booth, sipping and watching Jayvon get entertained by this big booty stripper chick who was looking a little too comfortable in his lap. He, Shylo, and Raj were all in on the three-way dance she was giving them, but there was something about how she was throwing her ass in a circle toward Jayvon that had me ready to throw my fist toward her.

As I sipped from my bottle of water, my eyes roamed Jayvon's eyes, hands, and even his midsection as ol' girl moved from his lap to Shylo's to Raj's. The little voice in my head was telling me to sober up, so I was. I wanted my aim to be on point when I drew my bitch from my bag to blast a bitch. Temptation is a muthafucka, and from the looks of it, Jayvon was falling into the trap of it.

When he felt me cutting my eyes into the back of his head, he turned around and waved me over to him. "Bring your fine ass over here, Morgan. It's about time you show your man some attention, don't ya think?" His question was more of a statement.

"Yup, daddy. I do owe you some attention so you can get your eyes off these hoes." I sounded spoiled, but I didn't care. Jayvon was my man, and if he was too caught up in temptation to let these hoes know, I would.

Walking up to him, I slid my hand inside his pants and rubbed on his manhood right in front of the girl. It was already semihard, which meant he must've been turned on by all the ass, titties, and pussy on display in front of him. A tinge of jealousy shot through me. No matter how often I'd parted my legs to a pretty bitch for Jayvon to watch and get pleasured, it was still a blow to my ego when he checked for another girl.

"A'ight, sweetheart, you can go." I twisted my nose up at her like she reeked and waved her off. "His main attraction is here, as you can see." I dismissed the stripper without even looking at her. When it came to Jayvon, he was mine, and no other chick was on my level. As soon as the girl was gone, she was off my mind.

"You're a trip, bae." He was laughing, watching the stripper walk away.

"Uh-uh, nigga. Trip my ass. I'm the truth, and I'll give it to you *and* her." Grabbing him by the chin, I turned his face from staring at her walking away to looking me directly in the eyes. "Hello? Do you understand?"

Instead of pushing my hand off him, he leaned in and kissed my lips, not answering my question at all. "Slide yo' feisty ass in that booth and calm down. Don't fuck up your night worried about a bitch that I ain't worried about. I love you and only you, bae."

Mad or not, I got my stubborn ass in the booth. I fell into his arms and sucked on his neck as soon as he slid in. Though I could smell the stripper's cheap fragrance, I didn't let it shake me to her level. Instead, I switched shoulders and kept clutching tightly to my man. It felt good being cuddled in Jayvon's arms and on chill. With our hectic lifestyle and love life, I know when to pause and enjoy the moment. Nothing perfect lasts forever.

Jayvon was in love with me. I didn't doubt that fact at all. He made sure his ass was home every night, protected me from harm, plus put me on a pedestal in several ways. In return, I pulled the strings to his heart, knew the depths of his soul, and connected to him like he was created just for me. It was Jayvon's dick that ended up being communal property, not his heart.

I threw back another shot just in time for the main event. The music stopped, and Nakeya's voice popped out of the speaker to announce her fashion show was about to begin. I cheered my girl on.

"Hey-hey-heyyyy, y'all." She was drunk and crunk. "I first want to thank all of you for coming out and sharing my special night with me. Then I wanna thank my homegirl, Morgan, for rolling with me and putting the bug in my ear to step up my game. It ain't nothing but love from me to this whole room. I ain't shit without my supporters." Though she was babbling and slurring her words, the genuine message was received.

The whole room clapped for and shouted kind messages up to her, like "You go, girl," "You deserve it," and "Congratulation." I couldn't help but smile seeing my girl grin and cry. She deserved all the praise she was getting.

Nakeya finished giving her speech, then announced the ladies she called "Keya's Angels." She'd gotten five strippers to model her line. Biting off the Victoria Secret's concept, it was cute, but these chicks were modeling for more than just support. They were twerking and working for a cash prize as well. The club was lit with supporters, and everyone, including Jayvon and me, was tossing bills onto the stage.

When it was all said and done, she bowed off the stage to a long line of girls excited to order. It was the perfect time to get a ripple effect going off the buzz she'd just put into the air, but instead, I had to run off Jayvon's cue. He wanted me to get the pills sold to the dancers before the last call for alcohol was made.

Chapter 9

Miranda

The ambiance at the club was exactly how I remembered it the last time I was on the scene. My head was spinning as I tried gathering my thoughts and positioning. I never ever imagined I'd be back begging for dollars with my body after Omari retired me. If I went back on the promise tonight by dancing again, I'd never be able to repromise him. That's why I'd started hustling with Amp and Dr. Basheer in the first place. My loyalty was with Omari in a major way. Whatever I owed him, I ultimately owed our son. I was trying to remain ten toes down on my word.

"Damnnn. My eyes must be playing tricks on me. Long time no see. How have you been, baby girl?" The bartender recognized me off the rip—and she should have. Candace opened the bar, closed the bar, and nursed all of us girls to the mental states we needed to be in to get butt-naked and nasty. She gave us liquid courage wherever it might've been lacking. Candace was the first person I saw whenever I worked at the club.

"I've been good. I can't complain. Still working the gig at the nursing home."

"I see." She nodded at my scrubs, which had to smell like Icy Hot and old piss. I really did do more than pass out Dollar-Store meds and fluff up charts.

I sank down on the bar stool, realizing I should've asked Shari to shoot me to the crib for a quick shower and clothing change. But it was too late, and I probably would've backed out anyway.

"So, what's up with tonight? Are you here to model for Keya?" She set a Styrofoam cup of liquor down in front of me.

"Nakeya, who be doing the custom clothes? Naw, I didn't even know about it," I took a sip of the drink and damn near fell off the stool. "Damn, boo. I see you're still heavy-handed as hell."

"Naw, baby girl, you're just a lightweight nowadays. Once upon a time, you'd be complaining over a wa-tered-down drink."

"Well, not tonight. Throw a few ice cubes off in this." I wanted the edge off but wasn't trying to misplace the mental discomfort I was feeling for a physical one. I hated being sick to my stomach off a hangover and having my body spazz out like the exorcist.

"Let me know if you ever finish this drink, and I'll check the back to see if we've got a Capri Sun or something." She was laughing so hard she could barely finish the sentence.

"Oooh, you ain't right. But I got you, and I'll check for you in a few." I laughed along with her, then tipped out before making my way to the locker room so I could check off into Shari for putting me in a trick bag. If Nakeya was throwing a party, I knew her entourage was in the building, including Amp and his bitch.

"Um, excuse me . . . but you could've told me who was having a party tonight." I walked up on Shari, clearing my throat.

"Girl, good the fuck bye. Since when are you worried about somebody's bitch? And from what you said in the car, you and Amp wasn't on nothing but some trickin' shit, and that's been over. Now, unless you were lying, I don't see what your problem is." She stopped talking and side-eyed me. Shari didn't know anything about me plugging Amp with pills.

"I wasn't lying. I just think you could've said something since you brought up Amp. But whatever." I got my outfit from the vending machine, then headed for the shower instead of taking an Uber home to my kid like my gut told me to do. Nothing about tonight felt right, but I downed Nita's drink, hoping it would drown all my anxiety. The water was cold since it was late in the night and had been in use all day, so I was in and out real quick.

"Okay, damn. My bad, Molly. I admit I didn't tell you intentionally. But why not let that nigga see all your sexy thickness and wanna trick that cash-cash off on you again? It ain't like you don't need the money. And besides, it's not like he's the only man up in here with pape'. Hell, it's some bad bitches out there with purses full of cash that's trying to trick as well. That CNA shit done fucked up your head when it comes to your hustle because worry is the last thing we do up in here when it comes to gettin' to the money."

"Awww, ho, shut up. I see you got jokes. You're not about to keep ragging on me about my job."

"Oh yes, I am." She burst out laughing, then poured half her cup of liquor into mine. "Now, hurry up and get sexy. His bitch just came in here, which means it's the perfect time for you to prey on him." Shari walked over to where Keya was sectioned off with her girls getting ready for the fashion show she was having.

It was then I realized Shari was actually walking in the show. She stayed paper chasing just as much as being on messy shit. I was at least happy for the heads-up that Amp was unattended to, though . . .

Jayvon

The club was going up, and me and my crew were living it up. We'd come a long way from being in juvie together, and it was only fitting that we got to flash our wealth. Keya had us in VIP, but we were laying out our own spread. I wasn't 'bout to drink, smoke, or mingle too long with any of my wifey's friends because I wasn't cut like that.

The crowd was still going nutty over Barz's performance, and he'd been ripped the stage and exited it. He'd brought the whole city out fa'sho. Nakeya was cool and had been hustling in the club long enough to have her own fans, but the hood-borne lyrical genius had all the ballers, goons, and hit men underneath the same roof.

"You did ya thang out there, homie. No wonder you're going from the hood to Hollywood." I gave Barz props, throwing my hand out there for a shake as soon as he returned to the VIP section.

"Thanks." He accepted my dap, then pulled me in for a brotherly hug. "Whenever you and the misses want a vacation, you know how to get at me. Ain't shit changing between us just 'cause a nigga got on with a contract and shit."

"I'ma hold you to that, bro. Real talk. I've been thinking about making an honest man of myself, but I ain't with all that hype involving a wedding. I might be able to talk Morgan into eloping in Vegas, then coming there for a li'l honeymoon."

"Dawg, no disrespect, but shorty must got magic between her legs to be lockin' you down like that. Wow."

"Wow is right. That's my baby. Let's make that the last time you comment on what's between her legs, though." What's understood don't need to be elaborated on. Barz knew not to take another step across the line all niggas know not to cross when speaking on another man's woman.

Barz and I got down together on the court back when we were youngins. Truth be told, he was a beast and had skills NBA players couldn't master. Barz and I used to go head up, one against one because there wasn't another baller in the hood worth our time to compete against. I'd sometimes rest in peace, him scoring more points and winning the game. And an equal number of times, I'd go in my pocket to pay him for whipping my ass in points. Little did I know I was funding the musical equipment he needed, one ten-dollar bill at a time.

Barz was never a gangster, thug, or delinquent in society. He worked at the neighborhood grocery store as a bagger, hooped whenever he was off work, and went to school whenever it was in session. I kept bullies from school off his back and niggas I hung with on the corners from stomping his head into the concrete because he wouldn't pick sides and join a gang. I've always respected his hustle of wanting to stay out of the way and do his own thang. It seemed like his way of thinking paid off, with a major recording deal on the line.

After a night of partying, Barz finally cut into me about purchasing some nose candy. That and a bunch of pills. The nigga was planning some wild shit with his weird-ass Hollywood entourage for the after-party at his private studio session, but I didn't judge nothing but the price. Because he'd purchased so much, I cut him a li'l deal. I'm about my money, not morals.

The waitress brought more bottles, beers, and drinks to the table. I'd been stopped paying. All the girls trying to get some attention from Barz were bringing free shit all night. Within a split second, he'd dumped a few bags of coke onto the table and had a gang of strippers in the booth performing like they were live in a music video. Every stripper that slid into our booth had to take a nose dip—his rule, not mine.

"Aye, these bitches here are bad. I'ont even know which one I'ma take home tonight. Real spit, it might be two." Shylo was thirsty, trolling for tricks.

"Dog, ya dick gonna fuck around and fall off behind you sticking it up in every hot twat twerking." Raj spoke up, shaking his head at Shylo in disgust. "Antibiotics don't cure every disease, ya know."

"Whatever, nigga. I straps up every muthafuckin' time. Ya better believe that," Shylo replied, pulling a roll of condoms from his pocket.

"Hell naw, fool." Raj burst out laughing. "Lemme hold two or three."

Me and the fellas kept taking shots and clowning. I was buzzing like a muthafucka waiting on my bae to get back from fuckin' with her friends. Tonight had been a good-ass night for us, and I couldn't wait to end it with my face snuggled between her thick thighs. Sliding back into my seat on chill, I wasn't even looking for no trouble, yet it found me.

"Yo, Amp . . . Ain't that ol' girl you fucks with?" Shylo low-key pointed toward a table near the bar.

"In the flesh." I quickly dug my phone out of my pocket and took her off my block list so she didn't disturb me and Morgan's time.

Me: Yo, wtf you here for? I shot her a text and watched to see how she was gonna play it.

A few seconds passed before she finally looked down at her phone, then looked right up at me, which confirmed she already knew I was in the building.

Randa: Trying to make some money. Wtf it look like? I could see her eyes rolling from across the room.

Me: Get your dumb ass over here now. I threw her back on block and put my phone back in my pocket.

Miranda

"You're so sexy. Where've you been all my life?" Dude I was giving a lap dance to was all over me for his ten dollars. I couldn't wait until the dance was over. I'd gotten chosen as soon as I exited the locker room.

All the money was in VIP, the main floor by the stage, and the sections where people paid for tables by the hour. Wasn't shit popping in the general admission section, and there never was. I hated working in that area, especially when I couldn't be the Goddess Girl I usually was. I used to own the titty club when I was in the game. That's why my baby daddy wanted me to sit down. I was about my bread and being about love humbled me. I couldn't even fall back into the groove of how I once was because I was lurking in the lame section, trying to stay out of Amp's way. His bitch's bestie had this place slapping. I hated when somebody counted my bag, but I knew Shari was about to be bragging in the car about her come-up.

I kept trying to busy myself with the dances I was giving, but I couldn't help but watch Amp and how he moved. I knew he was rude as hell with it at all times, but I couldn't help but be attracted to that same rudeness.

That's why when he hit my inbox up telling me to get my ass to his section, I was on it . . .

Morgan

"Girl, I swear you got some graveyard-ass love for your boo to be in here slanging some pills," Jos said, freshening her makeup in the mirror.

"I know we're homegirls, Jos, but what I do for my nigga is not your business."

I got extra irked by her calling out the obvious because it was what I'd thought about two or three times myself. Yet and still, it wasn't her place to speak on. I hadn't complained to her for her to feel she needed to have an opinion. "Yup, I do love his nut sac, and he fa'damn sho loves this juicy pussy. Now that we've got that understood, make that your last time making a reference to my nigga."

"Damn, bitch. I see the liquor's got you all in your feelings. I'ma shut up and get cute for the niggas out there looking to give a diva like me some more money to get cuter." She blew me off, turning back into the mirror.

I did the same, blowing her off and waiting on the few girls Nakeya told me she'd send in here that were certified pillheads. The quicker I got the pills off, the quicker I could get back to partying.

"Hey, are you Keya's friend?" A girl approached me, ass naked, carrying her costume and a bag of money.

"Yeah, I've got a pharmacy in my purse. Whatcha' want?"

"Okay, lemme get ten Ecstasy pills and your number to get some more." She started counting the money out of her bag, then handed it over.

I filled her request, plus passed my number over. I'd hook her up with the dealer later, whenever she called, but it was quicker to make money for now since I was trying to serve and move on.

Another couple of girls rolled up because of the first girl's reference, and then a few others who were lingering around. I noticed a few of their faces from being customers at my boutique but wasn't judging because all money made is good money to me. Jayvon was right. They were copping from me left and right so they could be charged up for all the dirty thangs that go on in the middle of the night. I was halfway out of pills by the time the last few of the girls Keya was sending in got to me. Although I really hadn't wanted to hustle here, it was too easy for me not to do it again. How ironic for Nakeya to come into my business to make money, and I was hustling out of where she just came from.

"All right, li'l Nina Brown." Jos called me when I was selling drugs. "Are you done yet? The DJ is playing my jam, plus I could be working up on some last-minute tips." Rightfully complaining, I didn't blame her. She was missing out on her coins being cooped up in here playing my bodyguard and shit.

Right when I was getting ready to tell my girl we could get back to the celebration because I was ready to pop my ass too, I saw the stripper that was twerking all over Jayvon staring hard at me. I mean, on the real, she was trying to get into my head and read my fuckin' thoughts. I'm super confrontational, so I didn't hesitate to ask ol' girl what was up.

"Um, so, it's obvious you want some attention. Don't waste it now that you've got it. Holla at me. What's up?" Walking up on ol' girl, I was heated and wanted her to feel it.

She laughed. "Honey, please. I'm walking around with a garbage bag of cash, not a grocery bag. I'm not lacking in the attention department, trust," she sneered, then hissed, "Yo' man can tell you how them niggas out there love this cat."

I snickered back. "Yeah, well, this bitch hates pussy cats. My man can tell you about that too. So don't get caught crossing in front of my muthafuckin' car in the middle of the night. Don't nobody blink twice about roadkill."

She laughed, disrespectfully amused by my threat. I'm not the type of person to warn a chick twice of what I'll do, so I let her continue talking herself into a bad fuckin' situation. And trust, she did.

"You can have your wordplay, mama. I'm on the clock. If you wanna continue this conversation, call me over to ya VIP section and tip a bitch to talk. I'll be bad for you and your boo."

"I'll snap ya neck," I growled, leaping for her.

Right on time, she backed into the locker, then slid past with a devilish grin. Jos had her arms wrapped around my waist, so I couldn't move with the bitch.

"Aye, you gotta come quicker than that if you trying to touch me, boo. This ain't the schoolhouse you're used to running, but the strip club locker room. Don't play a lion when you can't really rumble in the jungle." Ol' girl couldn't stop verbally coming for me.

I started elbowing Jos to get her off of me. "Get off. Damn. Let me at this ho." I was low-key about to try swinging on Jos for holding me back instead of helping me double-team the girl. The way I thought we rolled, real friends fight without a question being asked.

"Hey, baby doll." Jos got ol' girl's attention. "Ya mouth is gonna get ya ass served to you. I'm doing you a favor I really don't wanna do. If you keep talkin', I'ma let her go."

Not saying another word, she exited the locker room but not without giving me one last grin and wink over her shoulder. I was fuming, trying to pry Jos's fingers apart and from around me. All I wanted was to get loose with ol' girl. Whoever she was had gone too far and needed to be snatched back into place.

"Hey, Morgan, let that shit go and breathe. Our whole crew's been partying all night, and it's clear we're getting money to everyone in attendance. We probably shaded her about coming to our booth, and she's salty or something." Jos tried giving reason to ol' girl's behavior. "Don't ruin your night and all you've worked for over a peasant." It all made sense why Jos held me back, so I was glad I hadn't swung on her. She really was being a good friend.

"Thanks for looking out, sis. For real, I appreciate you, but I've gotta handle mine. You already know that. I'ma chill on that bitch for 2.2 seconds, but Jayvon, he's about to answer some questions right muthafuckin' now." Storming out of the locker room, I made a beeline for him and ended up grabbing a bottle while in tow.

Morgan

"Keya, Keya! Yo, Nakeyaaaa," I heard Jos call out for our girl, knowing I was about to shut the party down. I didn't play when it came to Jayvon—on my heart, soul, and life.

"For real, Jayvon? So, it's fuck me when you already know I told that ho to bust a move earlier?" I was talking to myself, charging myself up each step I took. You know how it is, ladies—when a nigga does some shit you just told him not to do, but he tests you like you're a weak link anyway. Yeah, *that's* how ya girl was feeling.

Through the strobe lights, over all the other heads partying, and through other bodies 'cause a bitch has telepathic vision when she's mad—I saw Jayvon having a damn good time. This time, the dancer had her titties

draped over his chest. She pounced up and down. Her
ass was jumping in the air, and only the devil knew what
she whispered in his ear. When his head wasn't bobbing
in between her breasts like a jolly-ass spoiled kid on
Christmas Day, it was tilted back with an expression of
pure enjoyment painted on it. He even had the audacity
to place his hands firmly on her booty cheeks like I wasn't
in the same building.

The VIP section has its own set of guards, and since
Barz and his Hollywood crew were drinking with Jayvon
and the fellas, his bodyguards were also surrounding
our section. I knew I couldn't run up on Jayvon and go
upside his head with the bottle. But I could be graceful
with it.

Slowing my anger, I put on a smile and tried to stay as
inconspicuous as I could so I'd catch Jayvon red-handed
and in action. The last thing I wanted was for ol' girl to
move. *I'ma teach her ass about quickness . . .*

I got up in the section. Raj and Shylo were too busy
getting their own dicks grinded on to warn Jayvon, so I
got a clear shot to clown. Raising the bottle to the side of
my head, I brought it down right onto the back of ol' girl.
Glass shattered all over her back, then flew everywhere,
even into Jayvon's face. I'd set it off.

"Yo, Morgan! Bae, damn," Jayvon yelled, caught off
guard by my surprise tantrum. He pushed the stripper
chick off him. She fell to the floor, shaking like a fish
out of water. She wasn't out cold, but I wished the slick-
talking, fast-dancing heifer was. After Jayvon shook the
glass off his clothes, he started moving toward me, but I
jumped back.

"Fair muthafuckin' game," I shouted, reaching to flip
the table over, making more of a mess between us. All the
liquor bottles, half-full glasses, and buckets of ice flew

everywhere. My adrenaline was pumping, and I was in rare form.

Barz and his crew trampled over ol' girl on their way out of the section. They didn't want no parts of the drama I was bringing, and I didn't blame them. A few other dancers twerking alongside ol' girl for dollars started running up like they wanted a piece of me, but Jos began to lay them out one punch at a time. I was so far deep into trying to get at Jayvon and the girl that I hadn't seen either of my besties come up. Whereas Jos was trying to battle bitches with me, Keya was only trying to break it up. This club was where she got her start, and disrespectfully, I was nuttin' up on her stomping ground.

"Raj, Shylo—5-o." I heard Jayvon's voice over all the chaos, followed by a few loud whistles. That was the hood call to tell hot boys to get the hell out of Dodge.

On cue, Raj and Shylo started breaking moves to get out of the club, and even Jos was moving toward the exit but dragging a girl by her hair along with her. Nakeya was trying to jump in the path of the security guards, who were off-duty police officers on the payroll of the strip club. They were heading our way. Drugs don't become an issue until the person carrying them does, so all of us needed to get ghost before we caught charges we couldn't get rid of.

As soon as I grabbed my purse from where I'd tucked it, Jayvon swooped me up out of the crowd and slung me over his shoulder. I was throwing my fists into his back and telling him to put me down, but he was trucking through the club, not minding one word of my rant. He didn't release his grip from my waist until tossing me into the backseat of his car. With the child locks on the doors, I couldn't climb over the seats and out the front door to protest leaving with him if I wanted to. So instead of trying to, I caught my breath until he slid in. Then I started laying haymakers into his ass. I was tagging Jayvon—all on the side of his face—the jaw, chin, and ear—until he swung back and knocked the wind out of me.

"Chill, Morgan. Damn. I can't believe you started all this bullshit over a stripper ho. The fuck, are you for real? Fuck yo' event? Fuck yo' girl? Fuck the fact that we've got dope, guns, and money on us? Huh?"

"Quit talking like you cared about tonight, Jayvon. Right before she hopped back in your lap, she talked slick to me in the locker room. That bitch ain't random, and I'm not dumb. Oh, and here's ya cut off what I made in the locker room while you were busy doing you—5 percent. I ain't ya bottom bitch, bitch. If you got time to pay hoes, you've got time to work and pay me better." I tossed a few handfuls of cash into the front seat at him, and he swerved and almost sideswiped a parked car.

"Aye, you know I ain't about putting my hands on you, Morgan, but quit tempting a nigga. And that's one hundred," he threatened me.

Looking at his facial expression through the rearview mirror, I fell back and settled down. Out of all the times we argue about him creeping around or even looking at a bitch with drool on his tongue, he'd never looked at me like he wanted to smack fire from me. He always let me go, and go, and go—knowing I was justified. The vibe I was getting tonight was totally different. I stayed quiet and stared out the window.

"I'm so tired of your disrespectful ass, Amp. I'm 'bout to be out here grinning in niggas' faces and see how you like that." I smirked, and he snapped.

"And on God, that'll be the last day yo' ass will have teeth in your mouth. Make me turn around and knock them pearly white muthafuckas down yo' throat if you want to, Morgan." His threat came with heart behind it. I knew Amp was serious, but I was too. I wasn't about to back down.

"Do you think I'm scared of you, Amp? 'Cause I think the fuck not. The last thing I'm gonna do is let you punch on me. I'll shoot the shit out of your black ass before I become a battered bitch. Now, drive and get me the fuck home before I piss all over this backseat." I'd gone from shaking mad to snapping my legs together like a toddler trying to prevent a spanking from having an accident. I couldn't wait to get from around his funky ass. He'd ruined my whole night.

The rest of the ride home had been quiet, which further indicated Amp was guilty of more than just tipping the stripper chick. It wasn't insecurity that was driving my anger but my intuition. Ol' girl didn't react like a jumpoff, but someone that was fuckin' with my man on a regular. My whole night had been ruined. I felt woozy, nauseated, and sick to my stomach behind the liquor and the truth.

Hey, y'all, just checkin' in. I made it home. Hope y'all are safe too. I dropped my status in the group chat and waited for the dots to pop up in the box that they were replying, but it was crickets. Either they were in their feelings, booed, or still caught up in the chaos at the club.

Setting my phone on the sink, I finished handling my business and washing my hands, then stripped down. The cold sheets against my skin and the cold air bumping in my room were going to help soothe the queasy feeling. The hot shower I was about to take would soothe the aches and pains from my fighting. This shit was for the birds. I had school in a couple of hours but was out here wilding in the club over a nigga that wasn't supposed to be community property. Ol' girl wasn't supposed to have a one-up on me. Amp was the one that should've gotten a bottle to his head.

At some point, I knew I had to stop fighting off bitches and put pressure on Amp to stop letting them in. He hadn't verbally admitted to anything, but I knew that stripper chick held more weight than he was being honest about. His vibe with her differed from any other jumpoff in the club.

I hated being mad. I hated letting my emotions get the best of me. But Jayvon drove me to act crazy. We had that toxic type of love that low-key had me wondering if I needed medication. After popping two Tylenol Extra Strength capsules and putting on my bonnet, I climbed into the hot shower, let it massage my pains for a few minutes, then turned the temperature down before I passed out from the saunalike heat. I was a water baby. It always soothed me. And the fat blunt I was planning on smoking straight out of the shower was really going to relax me. By the time my alarm sounded off for school, my whole mind-set would be different. I had no choice but to let this shit go for now.

After showering, I felt a lot better, and the tension headache was letting up. I checked my phone to see if the girls had dropped a line in the chat, but it was still crickets. I did have a message from Bryce, though, checking to see if I'd made it home safely. It was cute he was concerned.

Me: Yeah, I just did. That coffee, please make it an xtra large. LOL.

Him: I got you, party girl. Send me a pic of you partying before you doze off maybe . . .

I read the text a few times and thought about ignoring it, acting like I actually had dozed off, but since I was mad at Amp, I scrolled through all the pics I'd taken while partying, then sent him a few. He quickly hearted them and started typing back, so I sat on the edge of the tub, waiting for his reply.

Him: You are absolutely gorgeous. I won't bother you for any more. I only wanted to see how beautiful you looked tonight. Good night.

Me: Thank you (I inserted the blushing emoji), and good night.

I closed our messages with a slight smile, then walked out of the bathroom, ready for my weed-cap.

"Ugh, why are you in here, Amp? I *know* you don't think you're sleeping in here tonight. Take your nasty ass down to your man cave or maybe to that trick's house. I don't care." I tossed my phone onto the bed, then popped the cap to my lavender lotion and started working it all over my curves.

"The fuck, I *will* sleep downstairs tonight, just to keep from going upside your head." He rubber banded the money he was counting, then dropped the bills into a shoe box and slid it underneath the bed. "And if you keep talking gangster, I'ma pull off and let you stay up all night blowing me up." He then smirked like I was about to take the comment lightly.

But I tossed the lotion bottle at his head instead. "And I'll dead your ass in the morning. Quit playing with me, Jayvon Banks."

"Then quit playing with me and saying stupid shit you don't mean. It's late as fuck, and to keep it real, that shit you pulled at the club might kick a lot of heat back my way. Ol' girl wasn't just a stripper bitch—just to keep it one hundred with you. She was plugging me to some pills on the low." He finally exposed shorty's position, which made me angrier than I already was.

"Oh, so you're moving funny with your dick andddd the business. Okay, Amp. I see what tip you've been on. Since when?" I quickly slid on panties and snapped my bra in case I had to swing on him real quick.

"Shit, maybe a few months. And the flip has been hitting. All we've got going on is a moneymaking move, Mooka. Nothing more and nothing less."

"If it was nothing more or nothing less, you wouldn't have hidden the truth. But whatever. I also meant what I said earlier about matching energy, so prepare yourself. Now, get the hell out of my room and sleep on the roof for all I care. But if you leave this house, I'm putting a bullet in yo' shit as a parting gift. Good night, Amp."

"Good night, shorty." He walked out, shaking his head.

Miranda

Clutching my bag of prescription pain pills, I stormed out of the Urgent Care with more of an attitude than when I walked in. Partly because I had a li'l more energy thanks to the pain relief shot they administered. Amp's bitch really tried taking me out of the game tonight.

"Drive me straight home, and don't make no stops. And here's my bill. I want my cash within seven to ten days." I tossed my hospital bill at my homegirl as soon as I got in the car. I was mad as hell. I went to the club to make some extra cash and ended up in Urgent Care, cashing out for some stitches. This day felt like a setup from Satan.

"Aw, naw, bitch. This ain't my bill. You might wanna holla at Amp for that."

"I ain't got two words for that ho-ass nigga." I was openly in my feelings.

I'd blocked Amp from messaging me when I was in the waiting room. He wasn't blowing me up, but he'd sent a few messages asking me if I was straight and that he'd hit me up in the a.m. I knew he was busy catering to his girl, and his routine was to hit me up around her school schedule, but I was feeling extra alone in Urgent Care. They were taking forever because it was packed, and the idle time left my idle mind wondering.

"Okay, so you might not have two words for him, but we should slide past ol' girl's boutique and slide that bill in her mailbox." My girl was always up to start some drama.

"Girllll, bye. Like I said, take me home and don't make no stops. All I wanna do is curl up with my baby and forget all about today." I was pouting, damn near on the verge of tears.

I'd never been super emotional, especially in front of chicks from the club. Still, it was hard tucking my feelings since my baby daddy died, especially because they were often heightened or overexaggerated. I missed him badder than bad and was mad at myself for even being in the streets getting jumped when our son was at home with his moms. This was why he wanted me out of the club when I told him I was pregnant. He was trying to groom me to be a good girl. Shit could've gone even worse for me tonight.

Shari must've picked up on the vibes because she backed off. "A'ight, boo. I'ma get you home to your baby."

Chapter 10

Jayvon

I'd waited until Morgan's overly emotional ass was sprawled across the bed, snoring, before walking up the street to my mom's crib. In the state of mind Morgan was in, she might've actually tried popping a few at my ass. She was livid about ol' girl. And though I understand why she was tripping, her outburst might've fucked up me and Miranda's relationship. I'd hit her up a few times to see if she was straight, but she wasn't answering. All this shit was my fault for playing it so close, trying to have my cake and eat it too.

"Ma, hey, open the door up right quick. I'm 'bout to be at ya porch," I said, not waiting on a response because I'd use my key if I needed to. Flicking the cigarette I was smoking to the curb, I pulled the blunt from behind my ear and lit it while waiting for Valerie to open up.

"Oh, you might as well pass that here for making me get out of my bed." She reached for the blunt as I knew she would. "It's late as hell, Amp. What do you want?"

"Hit it hard. I ain't at ya door for nothing this late at night," I said, pushing past her, then giving her a few seconds to inhale. I sat on the couch, and she sat across from me and found her home within the buds. It was nothing for me and my moms to smoke together.

From the smell of cigarettes and smoke in my mom's living room, she didn't need another puff of weed. The slow-running fan, opened window, and burning candles weren't doing a thing for the stale smell. The smoke was embedded in the walls. Hell, when I lived here, the smoke used to be embedded in a nigga's clothes. I had to double bag and knot my gear up in garbage bags when I started getting a li'l money to jump Barz with for real.

"Whatcha' waiting on? Tell me. I know I look fuckin' fine for my age, but I need my beauty sleep if I'm ever gonna get a husband. I don't have all night to sit up with you."

"A'ight then. How you want it is how you'll get it. Jinx is home from jail and pulled up on me and Morgan at the trap earlier."

And just like that, I'd sent my wannabe gangsta-ass momma into a trance. Her eyes got big as saucers, her jaw dropped, and so did the blunt from her fingertips to the floor. She hadn't said one word, but I knew her mind was racing. My mom was the one who orchestrated Spencer's murder.

Jayvon—Back in the Day

"Boo, are you sure I can't tutor you in math and science? Maybe write your research paper, and you put it into your own words? That might be enough to pull up your grade so you don't have to drop out," Morgan begged, trying to come up with ways to make the principal and dean of students happy. "We did it before, and we can do it again."

Tears were falling from Morgan's eyes as she watched me clean out my locker. It was three o'clock on a Tuesday afternoon, and the principal of our high school had officially given me my walking papers. I'd been academically dismissed.

"Give it up, Morgan. It ain't shit, and I'm straight. I don't need a high school degree to crank up them dollars. Them dope kicks on ya feet and that diamond pendant on ya chest should be my truth enough that I'ma be one hundred."

I was doing more than saving face. I was keeping it real. The only reason I came to school daily was to hoop in central air or without gloves and sweats on in the winter. This school had a top-of-the-line court and workout equipment that murdered the street and community courts within the hood. Those are the only two things I was gonna miss about being a student 'cause I fa'sho as hell wasn't gonna miss walking a straight line around a bunch of uppity college-educated muthafuckas. They didn't relate to me.

"But what about Coach? Can't he help? Make a call or something?" Morgan wasn't taking no for an answer.

"Fuck that punk. He better hope the district don't start doing random drug tests with his dope-dabbling ass. He called in sick coincidently so he wouldn't have to be here when they dismissed me. But it's all good, Morgan. I swear it is. So hold up ya head. The only thing I need you to do for your boo is make that call when you get to Co-op class."

Propped against the locker, she sniffed like a toddler seconds after a whooping. I hugged and kissed her, then told her to call me as soon as the eighth hour was out. I couldn't keep Valerie waiting longer than I already had. My mom was outside waiting, and she was a bitch about burning her gas. I wasn't about to get my ass stomped for getting kicked out of school but for holding up her master plan. She didn't want me here wasting my time anyway. With me not having classes, basketball activities, or Morgan to cake with all day, my moms was about to set me up by setting up her boyfriend.

Valerie—Present Day

If Karma ain't a bitch . . .

Jinx being released from prison was a problem. A major fuckin' problem I hadn't anticipated.

Blowing the rest of my son's blunt down to a nub, I told his young ass to roll up another one. We were in some helluva real shit behind my decisions from back in the day. I wasn't the type of mother who coddled her son or kept him home at night out of the streets. I pushed him to get money, to protect himself, and to murder the nigga I was fuckin'. We had to eat, and the government's monthly cash and stamp stipend wasn't enough.

Spencer was my provider at the time. And when I tell you he had money on top of money that was stacked on top of dope, I'm not exaggerating or boosting his status. I'd watched Spencer grow from a bum to a boss, just the same as my son went from a bum to a boss. Funny how shit will boomerang back . . . Karma. Anyway, Spencer started slanging in the eighties, then took off, pulling up his rank in the eighties by pushing crack cocaine and heroin. By the time I had my son put him in a body bag, he had sold every dope the white man had made sure could reach the hood.

He and I were kickin' it strong for almost eight months before I orchestrated a plan to kill him. Spencer was giving me money for my rent, but I didn't have no rent. He was putting cash in my hand for whatever I asked for and was upgrading me from a rat to a hood-rich side piece. Spencer didn't have a woman or a wife but a bunch of bitches he was fuckin' on the front line. He tended

to all of us and didn't keep no secrets, but I didn't respect his honesty or care how he rolled. I'd always been a
woman with my own agenda.

From day one of Spencer rolling up on me, talking
about he'd look out for me and Jayvon in exchange for
me to letting him stash a li'l weight here and there, I'd
plotted on how to get down on him and come up.

The day Jayvon got kicked out of high school was the
day he killed Spencer. The plan was sweet. Jayvon's
uppity girlfriend called the truancy officer, flagging Jinx
(whose real name was Demetrius). The truancy officer
then picked up Jinx from his house, eventually turning
him over to the juvenile system because his fingerprints
came back with a hit of robbery and one of rape. I
knew Jinx was a problem child from snooping through
Spencer's drawers at home when he was showering after
one of our sex sessions. Spencer always got dumb and
went off guard after bustin' a fat nut.

Valerie—Back in the Day

"Damn, V. My dick drowning in ya bustin', sloppy-ass
pussy. I'm 'bout to come," Spencer moaned and grunted
on top of me.

"Hol' on, papa. Let me get mine first." I didn't care
about coming. I was only giving Jayvon more time to
man up and get his ass in this room. I'd told him to come
in when he first heard Spencer screaming about how
good I'm givin' it to him. But here we were, two minutes
into us fuckin', and Jayvon still hadn't shown me the
barrel of his gun.

"I can't. Oh shit, V . . . Ah." Spencer was reaching his
climax.

"Last stroke, cocksucker." I heard Jayvon's voice before the roar of gunshots.

Pow, pow, pow!

Three shots silenced the sexual moans that filled the air just moments ago. Even though I'd been waiting for them, they shook my body frozen like I was the one who'd caught the hot bullets. My boy really had it in him. He really pulled the trigger for his mama. My mind started racing as I tried to pull together the plot I'd stayed up countless hours into many nights, knowing that one day soon, I'd catch Spencer slipping to slip his riches from him. Ain't nothing deadlier than some good-ass pussy. As Spencer's heavy body went limp on top of me, it sprang me from shock, and I started trying to push him off my chest so I could at least breathe. His 300-pound body was going to crush me.

"Help get him off me," I mumbled out to Jayvon, who was standing there looking stupid with the gun. I guess I could only expect his young-minded ass to do so much. I was gonna show him how to finish a job, though.

We worked together to get Spencer flipped off the bed onto his back, making soft grunts of pain escape his lips. This big bastard had the nerve to still breathe faintly after taking all three bullets to the back. Air was still creeping into his lungs as we watched his chest slightly contract. Me and Jay were both waiting on him to take his last breath, but he was fighting through the attack. As big as he was, I thought the bullets were burning through his flesh because there wasn't a lot of blood. There was just a little splatter on the sheets and bedspread from where they pierced his skin with impact.

"Yay-you ddd-dirty bbb-bbitch." Though his breathing was shallow, Spencer still found the strength to spit venom at me. And though I deserved it, I wasn't trying to hear shit. I finally had the upper hand.

"I'm the dirtiest of them all, my baby. I've finally got one-up on you, and it's a major flex." I celebrated his downfall.

The look he gave me was cold, full of hate and resentment. Without a doubt, I knew he was regretting the day he first slid up in my snatch. He was a boss, feared by some of the deadliest goons in the city, but was being taken down by a poor bitch from the projects and her kid. I was about to grow Jayvon all the way up.

I lifted Jayvon's shaky hand. He fought with a bit of resistance, but I forced his wrist upward till it was aimed toward Spencer's heart.

"Ma . . ." Jayvon's voice got caught in his throat because he knew questioning me was a mistake. I didn't play when it came to it being us against the world. If it weren't for me, he wouldn't even have a life.

"Pull the muthafuckin' trigger." I patted him on the back, then winked at Spencer as the bullet flew into his soul. His death meant me and my son were about to be set for a very, very long time.

"What you've just done is some grown-man shit. This solidifies your spot in the game, and if we play it right from this point on, you can be bigger than this muthafucka ever was. Just make sure you stay on your toes at all times. Case in point proven." I stepped over Spencer, grabbed his wallet off the nightstand, then hurried up and dressed so we could finish the mission.

Since I'd snooped through Spencer's house before, I knew several of his hiding spots. So it was a quick grab of dope and cash before me and Jay were into the night like ghosts. And after his body was put into the ground, I had

Jayvon step to the streets with his sidekicks (my sister's son, Shylo, and their friend, Raj), putting the stolen product to sale. We'd been gravy ever since.

Jayvon—Present Day

After a few silent minutes, Valerie responded like only a true OG would. "You ain't got no other choice but to dead the nigga, son. Just like ya did his daddy. We got on by doing some dirty shit, and to protect our come-up, we've gotta get even dirtier. If that boy is anything like his father was, he's dangerous and will build up on your back. You remember what I told you . . ."

Cold and direct, my moms was just as cutthroat and grimy when she'd told me to set his dad up in the first place. She knew he would eventually leave her, so she put a claim on his riches before he had the chance to take away the help he was offering. We used the cash we stole to survive and buy more product, then sold Spencer's product along with what we'd purchased from a new connect.

"Damn, straight like that?"

"Yup, you already know how I am. And you already know a few of Spencer's friends from back in the day came pointing fingers at me and shit. Jinx ain't come holla at you for nothing, Jayvon. History must repeat itself. I ain't raise you to be no dummy, so I don't know why you didn't kill him on sight." Looking at me half motherly and half like the rider she'd been back in her heyday, Valerie was dead serious about me killing off another generation of the Weems family.

"Well, OG, make no mistake about it. He'll be dead on the next one. Gon' and take ya ass back to bed. I'm out."

Chapter 11

Morgan

Although I was tired as hell and barely holding on to the lecture, I was present. Professor Harris was serious about teaching us college-level students the importance of following through on the particulars. As a successful entrepreneur herself, she knew firsthand what it took to make it. I admired her from afar, respecting her whenever I came to class.

I was enrolled in a marketing course that met twice weekly and early Saturday morning. Out of nowhere, about six months ago, I decided to try my hand at school since I'd given it up after graduating from twelfth grade. It didn't start off with me enrolling with the ultimate goal to earn a degree or be a full-time student, but I was eight classes in so far. If my parents were talking to me, they'd be happy to know I was finally on the path toward an associate's degree . . . after they finished shaming me for wasting my life on a thug, that is.

I was always considered intelligent and to have potential, just easily distracted. All the teachers who told my parents that concern ended up being dead on the money. Had their premonitions told my parents the disturbance was going to be a knuckle-headed li'l nigga, they would've knocked the eyes out of my head and sent me to boarding school. I got attached to Jayvon at 17 and had been hooked on his thuggish ass ever since.

I was honest enough with myself to admit that a lot of the reason behind my not going to school four years ago was because of him, but I was ultimately in this seat right now because of Jayvon as well. On my twenty-first birthday, he gifted me a boutique along with bands of drug cash to get it stocked. It's funny how things work out.

Sassy & Classy was my baby, and I'd been investing a ton of time grinding to get it competitive in the market. It was making a profit every day I opened the doors, but it was far from what I envisioned. Thanks to all the extra tips, tricks, and ideas I'd been learning and implementing within the last year, though, it wouldn't be long before I was a mogul in my own right . . . with the help of my study partner, that is. Bryce was what you'd call an overachiever. He was the exact type of man my mother and father wanted for me. He was always the first in class, the last to leave, and the go-to guy if you ever wanted to be a part of a winning study group. No one but him knew the real reason behind him being so studious, but I was grateful for his consistently winning ways.

I had a whole separate personality, lifestyle, and list of morals when I was in school. No one here knew about my street life. Since I attended a community college outside of my district, I was a stranger to all the staff and students. All they knew about me was what I presented to them, and half of the stuff was lies. I might have rebelled against the uppity way I was raised, but I didn't deny it. I knew how "the other side" viewed loudmouthed ghetto girls with no class. My peers, counselor, and all the professors I'd crossed paths with so far would never believe I was a trap queen because I knew how to camouflage my bougieness. My acting skills were so good that they'd probably grouped me along with Bryce as an Uncle Sam. We'd definitely been labeled tokens for sure.

By the time I was finished with my thoughts, the professor was diving into her lecture on reading statistics. My ears were tuned in, and my fingers were moving in shorthand across the paper so I wouldn't miss a word of notes. My grade depended on it.

Fighting off a big yawn, I took a huge gulp from my Starbucks coffee and tried focusing my narrowing eyes. I was exhausted, damn near barely functioning. Though the Tylenol helped, I was still slightly hungover. I don't know which drained me more between partying, arguing, and fighting. I felt like a zombie when I woke up alone that morning.

The alarm on my phone, like clockwork each Saturday, went off at 6:55 a.m. It took me fifteen minutes to drag myself from bed, then ten to slide on my clothes and brush my teeth. I was glad it only took me a few minutes to find Jayvon passed out from liquor and weed in his man cave since I had to be in class by 8:00 a.m. A fifth of Raj and a bag of open buds beside him told the story of how he'd gotten down once we got home. I was glad to know he hadn't gone back out.

Buzz, buzz, buzzz.

The vibration of my phone interrupted me and every student around me. The professor's eyes darted around the room to see who was disturbing her lecture. Then they landed on me. I was flushed with embarrassment.

"Sorry," I quietly apologized, then dug into my purse to find and silence my cell. It was Jayvon calling. I couldn't answer even if I wanted to, but I didn't. I'd thought him up.

"Class, when entering my lecture room, give me the respect of having your full and undivided attention. Matter of fact, show some respect for both me *and* your peers. It is selfish to halt their learning experience. With that being said, refer to the syllabus for my policy on cellular devices."

Professor Harris might've been speaking to the whole class, but she'd directed her chastisement specifically at me. Her heavy-on-the-rag acting ass had me on the spot, and I didn't like it. It felt like I was in middle school all over again, and Lord knows I was far removed from having the innocence of a child. It took everything in me to bow out and nod, letting her know it wouldn't happen again. I hated being silenced.

The moment she turned her back to write on the board, I peeked at my phone, seeing a few messages Jayvon had sent that were still coming over. He was pissed as hell about me ignoring him, acting like I didn't have a reason to be still mad from last night. I wanted to text him back so-so bad, but I wasn't trying to get confronted by Ms. Harris again.

Class went on around me for almost an hour longer. It was beyond hard to focus. I almost wanted to leave, making myself fall further behind, but I fought against that choice. I wanted to stop putting his needs before mine. Though it was hard, I copied all the notes and tried holding on to the professor's words, at least to write them down. I'd worry about studying and processing what I could recall later.

My classmates rushed from the lecture hall, all needing a break from the many Excel charts, spreadsheets, and graphs Ms. Harris used to prove how certain advertising strategies worked better than others. I, however, used ten of those fifteen minutes allotted for break time taking pictures of all the slides.

"Um, excuse me, Professor Harris." I hated interrupting her.

"Yes. How may I help you, Morgan? I see you haven't taken advantage of break time."

"That's because I wanted to make sure I had all the notes copied. The call I interrupted the class with earlier was of an urgent matter that I must tend to. I won't be here for the second half of your lecture," I informed her.

She wasn't owed an explanation since this was college and I was free to leave, but it was more beneficial for me to have one-on-one relationships with my professors. My time, money, and future were on the line. Being the rebellious chick I'd been groomed into being by Jayvon wasn't the right role to play in this case.

"You'll be missing quite a bit of information." She looked up at me from over the rim of her glasses. Her expression read one of disappointment.

Professor Harris didn't know the particulars about me, but she was very well aware of my goals. As abrasive as I was in the streets about ma'fuckas giving me my money, I was just as assertive in class.

"I know, but I'll arrange to get what I'll miss."

"Very well, Morgan. Just remember—you must show up to be successful and fruitful."

If only she knew that's exactly what I was doing. I fa'sho knew all about the art of showing up. Since enrolling in school, I'd been semi-mastering the skill of being in two places—damn, three, plus the boutique—at the same time. I might've been attending community college for a degree in business, but I was already a mogul when it came to successfully running an illegal operation. Between the trap houses Jayvon and I were running, we were stacking Ms. Harris's annual salary in a week, if not less. Like I said, I too knew about showing up.

"Thanks, Ms. Harris. Have a good evening."

"You too. Hopefully, you'll be able to grace the class with your presence in a couple of days." She sarcastically ended our conversation, toting just as much attitude as she did intellect.

It took a helluva lot to bite my tongue. Had she been privy to knowing the *real* me, she would've walked on eggshells when it came to giving me the utmost respect. But I had a whole separate personality when I was in school, which was why I attended a community college way outside of my district. It made it easier for me to blend in. This was the bland lifestyle my parents wanted for me, just at a four-year university of their choice.

Grabbing my belongings, I rushed from the lecture hall as some of my classmates rushed back in, ensuring they weren't late. I was pissed that I had to leave because that meant I'd miss out on the study groups that were arranged after every class. This was the wrong time for shit to pop off at home. The student center was bustling, making my head spin even more, trying to find Bryce. I needed to ask for the notes and if he could sign me up for the study groups this weekend. I was becoming drained trying to be the studious student and the hard-core hitta at the same time.

"Bryce, hey, over here." I spotted him coming from the coffee station and waved him my way.

"Hey, are you about to check out for the day?" He walked up, taking note of my backpack in hand.

"Yeah, there's a problem at Sassy & Classy I've gotta handle," I lied. "Can you do me yet another favor and please send a copy of the notes after class?"

"Sure. You know I've got you. And if you need a tutoring session, I've got that covered too. Just let me know." He closed in on my personal space, and the cologne he wore danced underneath my nose, making my coochie tingle a li'l bit. Regardless of whether I wanted to admit it, there was an undeniable magnetism between us.

I froze. "Umm, the notes will be good for now."

"Are you sure?" He pulled me deeper into his orbit with his warm eyes.

It's like time stood still as I took in his confident smile, chiseled jawline, and the compassion pouring off him. I chewed on my lips at the unfamiliar attraction that was surging through my body.

"Yeah, well, umm, maybe. I might," I stumbled over my words. *Why are you tripping? What the fuck is this about?* I questioned myself, wondering if this reaction to Bryce was because I was pissed off at Amp.

"Well, just let me know. I'll catch up with you when class ends so I don't get locked out of the lecture hall." He leaned in and pecked my forehead, then rushed off against time.

Though the student center was still crowded, it seemed like I was the only one in the large space, lost in the soft kiss that Bryce had left behind. Though it was friendly, it felt like much more. Maybe all the innocent flirting wasn't so innocent after all.

Buzz, buzz, buzzz.

My cell phone vibrating against my hip snatched me out of my thoughts. It was Amp calling again. I didn't want to answer, but I knew not doing so would surely send us into war.

"Yeah, Amp. Damn. You know I'm in school," I snapped.

"Ay, yo, I don't give a fuck. And you're gonna have to quit that muthafucka if you can't answer the phone when I call," he went off. "I ain't with all that send a nigga to voicemail and ignore me shit you keep pulling and thinking is cute. A nigga can't get a lap dance, but you can be MIA? Naw."

"Don't you dare compare the two. They ain't the same. You got some nerve throwing that stinking pussy bitch back up in my face, especially when I'm out here on some boss shit trying to better myself. I should go back into class and leave your black ass at home stanking till I'm done," I threatened, knowing I couldn't go back into class if I wanted to because the door was locked by now. Plus, I wasn't sure I could stand being around Bryce at the moment.

"If you're not home in twenty minutes, it's gonna be a massacre at that school, Morgan. You know I'll blow that bitch up behind you. Don't play with me."

"Naw, maybe you should stop playing with *me*. You wanna be a bomber so bad but won't treat me right. I'm tired of your shit, Jayvon." I went from being lost in my emotions about Bryce to screaming about how hurt I was to Jayvon. I definitely needed to smoke and calm my nerves.

"Maaannnn, shut that shit down and get to the crib, Morgan. You know a nigga love you and only you. Quit tripping 'cause there's something on the floor I need to talk to you about. I'll see you in a minute." He hung up like his pep talk was enough to ease my rushing heart.

"Oh my God, this nigga is draininggg me." I hit the steering wheel and cried out into the car, hating that our love story was so toxic.

I found myself wondering what a bland lifestyle really would really be like . . . with Bryce, though.

Chapter 12

Morgan

"You've reached Nakeya, but I'm not available right now. Please leave me a brief message, and I'll hit you back." Her greeting played in my ear for the fourth time in a row, so this time, after the beep, I went ahead and left a message. If Amp wasn't waiting at home with an attitude, I would've popped up at her crib for a face-to-face conversation. I'd been calling her since I pulled out of the parking lot at school, hoping that apologizing to her for last night would be a distraction from the thoughts of Bryce that were invading my mind.

"You know who this is because you keep sending me to your voicemail. I understand if you're pissed about last night, but you can at least pick up and let me explain what popped off. We're supposed to be better than that. You know I wouldn't wreck your shit without a good reason or at least a good apology afterward. I'm woman enough to admit I owe you that. Answer the phone or call me back." The voicemail cut me off, so I went ahead and hit send. I was done begging and wasn't about to keep blowing her up to keep getting ignored. I might've let my feelings get the best of my decision-making skills last night, but it wasn't like she hadn't been through the drill at my shop before. A few bitter chicks had popped up at the glamour bar on bullshit behind them beefing, but I looked past it because I thought our bond was better than that. I was hoping I would get a callback from Nakeya so we could get back on track. But until then, I had to deal with Amp. I was finally arriving at home.

When I pulled into the driveway, he and Raj were posted on the porch, blowing some backwoods. I could see the thick streams of smoke drifting into the air. I swear the only reason he didn't want to move from the hood is because he liked doing hood shit. We had a whole backyard set up like an oasis, but he'd rather be on the porch blasting music and getting high.

As soon as Jay and I locked eyes, he went from vibing to the music to griming at me. We started having an unspoken conversation that was heated as hell. And I guess Raj picked up on his tension because he looked between him and me, shaking his head, then nodding it into his phone. Raj knew better than to get in between us arguing. Everyone knew it was better to let us iron out our shit than get in between it 'cause once we got back on good terms, it was us against the world again.

"Hey, Miss Morgan," Popps greeted me, opening the car door and grabbing my book bag.

"Hi, and thanks a lot, Popps." I acknowledged the fact he'd been a gentleman before sassing Jayvon. "Damn, you could've opened my door since you're only a few feet away. It's the little things, Jayvon. The little fucking things," I complained.

"Girl, shut your bougie ass up. I ain't got time to do li'l petty shit because I'm too busy doing big shit like paying your tuition. Hell, I paid for that nigga right there to open your door. Don't come home with that bullshit, Morgan."

"I'ma come home how I want since you were blowing me up like it was a 911 emergency." I stomped out on the porch, leaned back against the rail, then glanced at my Rolex, gesturing that time was of the essence. "Tick-tock, crybaby. What do you want?"

Amp jumped up, but not as fast as Raj jumped in between us.

"Whoaaa, li'l sis. You're about to get knocked in the bushes. Please don't do this." He was barely holding Amp back. The veins in Amp's forehead were bulging. He was ready to flex my ass across the rail, fa'sho. I knew it. "Y'all know I don't wanna be in the middle of y'all business but can't leave y'all scrapping."

"I'm good, G. Good looking, though. Do me a solid and run that package over to Dex for me, then fall back through here." Jayvon might've been talking to his homeboy, but he looked directly at me.

I stormed into the house while I had a chance to get some leeway.

"Bring yo' ass back here and sit down. We need to talk." Jayvon came into the house yelling after me.

"Fuck you, Jayvon. You weren't trying to talk a few seconds ago when you were fronting me off in front of Raj. I swear to God—whenever I'm in class, you pick a fight with me. Like you can't handle me doing me. Like you can't handle me getting a degree and running a successful business."

Jayvon's nose flared, his eyebrows curled into a frown, and his temples started thumping. "What I *can't* handle is your ass being ungrateful. Not only did I give you that boutique you make money off of, but I also paid your tuition. Fuck out of here with that 'I can't handle you doing you' bullshit. I made yo' ass on every level."

"Yup, you're right, Jayvon . . . You made me."

As I took aggressive steps toward him, he straightened up his stance, bracing himself. He knew I'd pounce on him like an alley cat from many previous fights over the last nine years. The temptation was intense for me to buck at him, but I didn't. I yanked the blunt he'd put to his mouth out of his hand instead. "The only thing you make about me is sick. Believe that, jerk." Storming off to our room, I didn't stop and turn around when he called for me to. "You can kiss my fat ass, nigga."

Jayvon got on my nerves. That's because I loved him so much. Otherwise, his opinion and the shit he talked about wouldn't have mattered so much. I was tired of him throwing up what he'd done for me in my face. In my opinion, I'd earned the boutique, my tuition payment, and even my stripes as a hitta. I'd had his back for so long that I felt *he* owed *me*.

Sitting on the side of the bed, I smoked the rest of his blunt down to a nub. I wanted to grab the bottle of wine from the fridge I'd started on last night but didn't want to leave the room. I could've stayed at class and gotten the full lecture for all this nonsense we were going through. The more I thought about what I was missing, the angrier I got. I couldn't figure out why sometimes things went good with us, then tart and sour the next.

Lying back, I stared at the ceiling, letting my mind wander off. Since I'd only smoked a fourth of a blunt, I only felt a slight buzz and knew it would pass shortly. As bitter as I felt, I wanted to enjoy each moment of the intoxication but couldn't. Jayvon's words were still cutting me where it hurt. Between the two of us, he was the one who should have been tagged as ungrateful. I might as well have spit in my parents' faces behind choosing him over them. Right when I was about to go to his stash to roll up a fat one, he knocked on the door.

"Yo, open up so we can talk." He sounded calmer, but I didn't care. I wasn't in the mood to be bothered.

"Go away, Jayvon. You've said enough—trust me," I responded, caught in my feelings. "I ain't trying to hear shit else that can quite possibly come flying from your smart-ass mouth. Between last night and now, I need a break."

"C'mon now, bae. Don't be like that and make shit worse. You know I'll kick the door off the hinges if you don't open it up," he threatened.

"I don't care. Do what you've gotta do."

Jayvon was always up for the challenge. Seconds later, I heard his foot meet with the wood of the door. Two swift kicks later, the frame cracked, and the door swung open. He'd broken down the barrier I'd set between us.

Sitting on the bed with my legs pulled up to my chest, I looked at Jayvon dumbfounded while shaking my head. "Are you happy now?"

"Yup, I am, as a matter of fact. Popps can have a new door up within an hour. He looking for some extra work anyhow." Stepping over the broken wood chips, he made his way over to me. "I knew you were in here mad, and I ain't want you pissed at me. You know I hate when we're beefing." He looked up at me with puppy dog eyes. This was the side of Jayvon no one in the streets ever got to see.

"Well, I don't know what to tell you, Jayvon—other than quit making a problem of me going to school." I refused to back down, though I wasn't going to bring the stripper chick back up at all. She was a minion, a nonfactor, and not even a thought in the grand scheme of my future. I'd given up getting my degree once for the love of the hustle. Now that I was actually in the thick of my courses and making connections with my professors, I didn't want to let the opportunity go again. "For real, Jayvon . . . Why you always gotta go from zero to one hundred whenever school comes up?"

Sitting on the bed, he pulled the blunt he must've rolled when I rushed in here from behind his ear and lit it. "'Cause . . . as soon as you get yo' degree and shit, you ain't gonna be trying to trap with a nigga no more. I know I got Raj and Shylo, but you're the mastermind behind us being able to stack so much money while opening more spots. You already acting funny, so I can only imagine how shit really gonna be like when you're done getting your degree."

I didn't know what to say. Jayvon was laying his feelings on the line. And I finally understood his side of things for the first time since I'd enrolled in school. The part of me that loved him more than I loved myself humored giving up school. I'd lost love with my family and invested too much into our relationship to let us fail as a couple. As far as I was concerned, Jayvon was my future, and I was totally confident in saying that without a ring on.

"I don't see how I'm acting funny, babe. You ain't never had to worry about me creeping with another nigga. I'm still shooting moves and handling the trap spots, plus the boutique, and I'm still the baddest bitch in bed, according to the sounds you made last night. If anything, I'm only bettering myself for you and us. I might not trap with you forever, but I'm fa'damn sho gonna be with you forever."

"That ain't good enough, Morgan. I'm a hood nigga. I popped out of a hood chick's pussy, and I'm gonna get buried by a bitch that's married to the hustle the same way. I want that to be you, but you got different goals and shit."

"My goals don't change who I want to be with. If anyone is acting funny, it's you. I can't believe we're having this conversation." At first, I was a little hurt behind Jayvon thinking I'd play him, but the more he spoke on the subject, the more I realized this was just another 'all about him' moment.

"Naw, that ain't me, Morgan. I'm still chopping it up heavy on the block day in and out while you're at school or gossiping with your girls at that damn boutique. I know you're not trying to hear this, but you're gonna have to make a choice in the near future."

I lost my cool. "A *choice?* Wow, Jayvon. You're selfish as hell. I've been choosing you. My moms don't fuck with me, my dad follows her lead, and not even your ratchet-ass momma can accept me. Don't ask me to choose between you and school because you won't like it." I'm not sure if I meant what I was saying, but it felt good threatening him with conviction in my voice.

His phone rang, as always, and I got irked on instant.

"Aw, hell naw. I know you're not about to answer that phone while we're talking," I snapped, jumping up from the bed.

"Back up with all that ra-ra shit, Morgan. We ain't talking. You already told me what I needed to know," he said indifferently, throwing his forearm up, blocking me as I walked up into his space.

"What's that supposed to mean? Quit talking in riddles." I kept pushing up on him.

"Yo, back up for real." The bass in his voice had increased. "I ain't talkin' in no fuckin' riddles. You don't wanna choose between me and school, so I ain't gonna make you. I'm about to roll out with the fellas, so we'll see what yo' love be like for a nigga when I get back."

With that, he pushed me onto the bed and got up to walk out the door. I started to run after him, but my pride wouldn't let me. All I wanted him to do was fight for me. Instead, I heard him answering Raj, telling him he was walking out as he spoke.

When I heard Raj's car reverse out of the driveway, I jumped up, calling myself packing a duffel bag to leave. I had myself fooled too, especially reminding myself about the other night and how him not giving up the gang-banging lifestyle really might be a deal breaker for us. Those were thirty minutes of wasted time I'd never get back. I didn't even get my bag zipped before my clothes were unpacked and back in place. You know how one thing goes wrong, then a second, and is followed up by a third? I felt like my relationship with Jayvon was stuck in a whirlwind of problems.

Chapter 13

Jayvon

As soon as I stepped one foot out the door, I pushed the problems between us to the back of my mind. She had her fallback plan, but I was still deep into the game. And to add several layers of madness on top of it, I murdered Spencer to get my start, and now, I needed to find and murder Jinx to retire.

"Where to, Jayvon?" Raj played like he was an Englishman driver.

"Into war, so load one up top and have some ammo at ya fingertips." I kept it real, then gave him directions to where Spencer and Jinx used to wreck shit at. Raj pulled off without fear or question.

Thankfully, my left-hand man didn't need a reason to roll out alongside me or have my back without an explanation. Raj, out of us three, had the least to lose. He didn't have a woman, kids, or a family he gave a fuck about. Raj was thrown into the system by his mother when he was 13, as soon as he was old enough to go into the juvenile system. He was a knucklehead, the type of kid who did wrong for attention, regardless of how crucial the circumstances were. He was so crazy that muthafuckas really thought he was head-sick.

His mom got tired of taking him to psychiatric appointments, trying different medications that only brought out crazy side effects, and parenting him all alone. When Social Services started fucking with her, talking about making her liable for his behavior, she signed Raj over without hesitation and dropped him off to become a ward of the State. Manish-ass Raj became a menace to society instead. When he crossed paths with me and Shylo, we three became the wrecking crew.

"Yo, did you holla at Shylo or hear from him? Is he in Penny yet?" Caught up in my own drama with Jinx and Morgan, I hadn't touched base with my cuzzo.

"I'on't know. That nigga ain't like me. I do shifts of ten. Ten to drive there, ten to rest, then ten straight hours to drive back. You know ya cuz likes to pull over at rest stops and fuck with the truck driver prostitutes."

"Man, that nigga dick just might fall off." I referenced what Raj said the other night at the titty bar about Shylo fucking any chick walking.

We told a few jokes, caught up about the drama at the titty bar, and then prayed for protection from the sins we were about to commit. It didn't take long to get to Jinx's childhood neighborhood. He wasn't from our zone but only a few miles away in another roughed-up area. Back in the day, when there were picnics or local activities, our zones would hook up together but didn't linger together on a day-to-day basis. Folks from the hood are cut that way.

Raj drove at a moderate speed, waiting on his cue to aim and shoot. I told him a basic description of Jinx, but my eyes were roaming enough for both of us, plus Shylo in his absence. I wanted to kill Jinx so bad that I'd imagined it time and time again. Block after block, I made eye contact with every man that was outside. If Jinx was around, he wasn't making himself seen. And just because I didn't have eyes on him didn't mean he didn't have eyes on me.

I was fidgeting in my seat, antsy to find Jinx and murder him. I was mad at myself for not murdering him the other day when he first popped up on the scene. That shit was an amateur mistake. I wouldn't be miscalculating my steps again.

"Yo, pull over at that store real quick so I can grab a li'l two-dollar shot or something," I spoke with frustration. As long as Jinx was alive, he was a problem. Sliding my pistol into the waistband of my pants, I was prepped to get out fully protected, but Raj stopped me.

"Jayvon, man, fuck that liquor, bro. I been on both you and Shylo's team since a nigga was an absconder, which means I know when some shit ain't right with either one of y'all. What's good, for real? It don't matter whether you're wrong or right, you know. I'ma rock and bust bullets with you, dog."

"Raj, real spit, if I could kick it with you about the shit, I would." I sounded like I was carrying a ton of weight on my back.

"And you can. Not on no homo-thug shit, but on some, 'I roll with this nigga, and he's my brother' shit." Taking a breath and a break from speaking, he slammed his hand on the dashboard, then said, "Fuck it. Look, man, I know I'm the last cat to care about family off the strength of how my momma played me, but that's what makes me value you and Shylo like family. At the end of the day, if we can't rap with each other and hold one another down on all levels, we ain't gonna be shit but some washed-up hustlers in the long run."

No matter how tough my exterior was, Jinx's appearance had fucked me up. Raj and I had history and were like family since he'd been around, but if he was seeing through the bullshit and noticing something different going on with me, then I was moving differently on all angles. I had to tell him the truth about Jinx. The only part I left out was that Mom Dukes put the play into motion.

After riding the city on a dry run, my homeboy took me to the mall to get Morgan an apology gift. The mall was buzzing as it was Saturday afternoon, so I was hoping I didn't bump into anybody. I was trying to be in and out.

"Yo, what it do, sis?" I said, answering the phone.

"Nothing. Is Morgan around you?" Nakeya was whispering.

"Naw, what's up?"

She smacked her lips. "You know I'm mad about how she clowned last night, right? I mean, I don't know how hugged up you were with Molly because I didn't see it, but Morgan fa'damn sho didn't have to throw a bottle."

Dropping my head, I instantly regretted that I'd answered Nakeya's phone call. I'd only done so thinking Morgan was with her, or something might've been wrong. By no stretch of the imagination did I expect anything petty. I didn't want to get caught up in no female catty shit, so I told her just that. I'm not her nigga to care about how she feels at the end of the day—bro and sis or not. "Naw, sis, I didn't know, but I'm sure you and Mooka will work out whatever it is. You know how y'all link up and shit."

She sighed. "Yeah, whatever. We probably will, but I'ma let her sweat it out until the boutique opens Monday. I just wanted you to know what was up just in case she brought it to you that I wasn't answering."

"Man, see, that's why I don't get mixed up in chick shit. Besides y'all being friends or sisters—whatever y'all are day to day, you two are supposed to be getting that bread up, not beefin'." In the middle of their drama or not, I had to call Keya out. Messing with Morgan was the same as meddling with mine. Real talk.

"But, bro, that's what I'm saying. The owner got at me last night after the club got shut down and said if I keep doing business with Morgan, he's seriously gotta debate funding my clothing line any further. I know a bitch is getting her coins out here, but ain't shit like a good ol' sponsor."

At that moment, even salty over Morgan choosing school over a nigga so much, I was happy she was about her business. I couldn't imagine how far run into the ground I'd be with a basic hood rat looking for a handout and a nigga to pay their bills. It's different when you're getting help from your partner versus what Nakeya labeled as a sponsor.

"Hey, sis, at the end of the day, all I can say is, do you. But I'll holla at you later 'cause I'm in the middle of something." I ended the conversation, feeling I'd already let it go on too long. At the end of the day, whether Morgan was right or wrong, I was riding with her.

"Okay, bro, love y—"

I let her words get caught up in the click of me ending the call. Not only was I not getting ready to keep humoring shorty while she spoke ill about my wifey, but I'd also been rude to the salesman standing before me long enough.

"My bad, bro. Lemme grab this one and whatever upgrades it comes with. This is for my girl, and it's an apology gift, so make sure you get me set up straight." I pointed to the laptop I'd been seeing Morgan eying online.

"No problem. I'll take care of you. I just made up with my girl a few weeks ago with the new iPhone." He went down memory lane, knowing my current position all too well. "Give me a second, and I'll meet you at the register."

Pulling out my wad of cash, I got prepared to pay the tab. Raj came over from messing around with the computers. "Dog, if this don't make Morgan forgive me, I'ma kick ya ass, plus make you reimburse me for every dollar I'm about to drop."

"To hell you ain't. It's a hundred laptops in here, but ya bougie-ass girl would want the most expensive. Don't blame or hold me accountable for shit. You better save the receipt and bring that lavish muthafucka back if she don't want it. The most I can do is drive you."

Chapter 14

Morgan

Over an hour passed, and Jayvon still wasn't back. I was irritated to the max. Thankfully, my crew at the shop could hold it down in my absence. I very much so lied whenever I used the shop as my excuse to bail from school because everyone employed at Sassy & Classy was money-hungry paper chasers. They opened earlier than I woke up and closed down after I was in bed sometimes. They didn't need me to hold their hands or micromanage their grinds.

After I play-packed, I used the time Amp was forcing me to stay inside to study since I was supposed to be in class anyway. Pulling out my textbooks and the notes I'd taken in class before leaving, I dove right into the material. I even jotted notes downs along the way that were good ideas to implement for my shop. The more information I processed about marketing plans for my upcoming test, the brighter I believed my future could be as an entrepreneur. Even though many things would have to change before I could, I'd set a goal of opening up another location. It wasn't an impossible goal to attain either. Amp was just gonna have to get with the game plan.

Taking a break from studying, I pulled out the notebook I kept for Sassy & Classy and went over my to-do list as well as the numbers so I could do a deposit drop at the bank first thing on Monday morning. Then I restocked some hot items, ordered some new pieces, and did a media blast online. I was always working on improving Sassy & Classy's social media imprint and was considering hiring an assistant to help until the end of the semester. I was pulled in too many directions and starting to feel slightly burnt out.

My phone rang as soon as I got ready to start back studying. I thought it was Jayvon responding to my text about him feeling my wrath if he was with another female. But it wasn't. My caller ID read Customer Brielle, which meant it was really Bryce calling. He was stored under an alias to throw off Jayvon if he ever saw him calling. He'd knock my head in between the washer and dryer for giving a nigga my number, square or not. He'd swear all the times I didn't answer the phone during lectures was because I was cheating.

"Hey, Bryce." I hopped up out of bed and peeked out the blinds to make sure the coast was clear.

"Hey, is this a good time, or does the boutique have you tied up?" he questioned at the sound of my voice.

"Actually, you couldn't have called at a better time. I'm just getting in from taking care of stuff at work," I lied.

"Cool. That's good you've taken care of things. I know how important Sassy & Classy is to you. I'll shoot you over an email of all the notes you missed once I get home and scan them in. Just to give you a rundown, though, we covered all of chapter nine, part of ten, and the section of eight she's gonna let us retest on. The grades are posted from the quiz if you haven't checked."

"Wow, I missed almost a whole semester in one-half of a class session," I whined, opening another window on my tablet to check the site for my score. "I got a 73 percent, Bryce. A 73! I'm going to mess around and fail this class."

"You won't. Have some faith, baby girl."

"God ain't gonna bless a mess. I'm going to have to buckle down and possibly get an assistant to help me run things until the semester is over."

"That doesn't sound like a bad plan. You've put a lot into getting this far, and I'd hate to see you slip this far out into the semester."

"Me too. I'm most definitely about to buckle down and study so I won't tank the retest too."

That meant that Jayvon was gonna have to start delegating more and keeping his hands from getting as dirty as they did on a daily. Raj and Shylo should've been putting in more work when it came to running the traps than they were. At least until this semester ended, and I didn't care how he felt about it. I wasn't planning on choosing between school, my business, and the hustle that kept us. I'd been letting him have his cake and eat it too for years—and now it was my time to do the same. It was time for Amp to ride shotgun to *my* plans for a change. Fuck him talking about "seeing how real my love is," 'cause I'd already shown and proved my loyalty time and time again.

"That sounds like a good idea, baby. Procrastinating on hiring someone competent can only hurt you at this point. It appears Professor Harris will be flying through all she noted on the syllabus, plus more. I can tutor you on a few topics and, of course, look out with the notes whenever you've gotta miss class, but I just got signed up for a hectic schedule at work. I'm about to have a lot of sleepless nights myself."

Completely ignoring Bryce's complaints on his issue, I was too wound up in mine. We're only halfway into the semester, and anxiety was bombarding me. I was not feeling confident that I could pull off the complete one-eighty change that required tons of focus and time—

which I lacked tremendously with the help of Jayvon. A passing grade in this course was necessary to progress to the upper-level ones. Simply put, I couldn't get my associate's degree without passing this class. I felt extra screwed because it was too late to drop the class.

"Hey, you got quiet on me."

"Yeah, my bad. Just wondering if I'm gonna make it to the end of this semester," I sighed, being honest.

"Of course you are. That ain't even gotta be a worry of yours as long as I'm around, sweetie." Something about the tone of his voice settled me to the point of smiling. Bryce was always encouraging, but something about this time was different.

"Wow, for real? You've got me like that?" Pushing my notebooks and stuff to the side, I Indian-style folded my legs and caught a glimpse of myself in the mirror. My cheekbones were raised and red. Bryce's pretty nerdy ass had me blushing.

"Make no mistake about it, sweetie."

Sweetie? Since when . . .? And why am I . . .? I was confused and twisted up in my thoughts about when Bryce started using pet names with me because he'd always called me Morgan, and more importantly, why I was blushing by him doing so. I didn't hear Shylo pull back up in the driveway. Jayvon was already coming through the front door when I realized he was back. I was about to get caught doing whatever it was that I was doing, which I couldn't name 'cause I was not sure what it was, but I knew it was wrong.

"Morgan! Yo, Lia," Jayvon called out to me as soon as he entered the house.

"Hey, Bryce . . . I've got another call coming in. Can I call you back in a few?" I rushed him off the phone, hoping he hadn't heard Jayvon yelling crazily on my end.

"Yeah, sure. It's no thang, baby girl," he replied. "The email is—" I'd cut him off by hanging up.

Jayvon was two paces from the bedroom, and I wasn't about to let him find me on the phone with another nigga. He might've been crowned a cheater, but he'd never accept the same behavior up out of me. Right before he popped up in the door, I'd cleared the call from Bryce altogether.

"Hey," I huffed dryly.

"You still mad at a nigga, I see. Why didn't you answer me when I walked in but texted me some dumb shit?"

"For starters, yes, I'm still mad at you. And second, but most important, I didn't text you no dumb shit. Don't act like you haven't been caught slippin' with ya dick."

Jayvon sighed. "Not the fuck today, Morgan. Don't even start with a nigga." He cut me off and shut me down, then went straight for his stash and broke the buds into a fat blunt.

Although I wanted to know where he'd been at on the real, I kept my curiosity to myself. Pulling my spiral notebook up to my face, I tried memorizing the first few concepts on my page and taking my mind off him. My heart was heavy on Jayvon, no doubt, but Bryce's rundown of what to expect from Miss Harris's class had my mind somewhere else.

No matter how hard I tried to concentrate, I kept drifting off and daydreaming. Everything was a blur to me on the page. The tension between my man and me was too thick. I hated the fact that he cheated, but I understood why girls flocked to him. His body was toned, his dick was long and meaty, and his swag was on a million. Since he didn't have kids or a wife, bitches didn't care that he claimed me as a girlfriend. As far as they were concerned, Jayvon was fair game.

Jayvon fired up the blunt, then walked out of the room. Just as I was getting ready to have an attitude over him not saying anything else to me, he returned with a large gift bag, balloons, and a flower he'd probably gotten off the corner from a bum selling them. I wasn't judging his gesture because I'd been on his mind. It's always the thought that's more important. This was Jayvon's attempt to win forgiveness. I was happy to hear him out.

"A nigga fucked up, baby. Over the last nine years, I ain't did nothing but apologize to you over and over again, but I still ain't got the shit right. You know what it is between us, though." Handing me the bag, he let the balloons fly to the ceiling and set the flower on the nightstand. "The receipt is in the bag, just in case I got the wrong one. You know I don't know nothing about shit like that."

Pulling his apology gift from the bag, I was pleasantly pleased and surprised that he'd gotten me the top-of-the-line MacBook I'd been thinking about getting, a new iPad, plus some new sparkly cases. My eyes lit up. "Oh, wow, thanks so much, babbyyy! This was so thoughtful." I leaped into his arms and hugged him tightly. I'd been needing a new computer. He'd been paying attention. Jayvon getting me this gift meant he'd heard my complaints and was actually trying to accept me being in school.

"I'ma take all this loving you giving a nigga as you like it." Hugging me back tightly, he bit my lip, then moved to my neck and started sucking on it lightly. "Forget all that shit I said earlier, baby. I ain't trying to be a bitch or nothing, but thinking about you leaving me drives me crazy."

"I love you, boy. You ain't never gotta worry about me leaving you . . . but I'ma need you to start believing in me. I've shown you I'm in your corner. I swear that'll never change. We're supposed to be settling more with each other the more years we share, not drifting apart."

He hugged me tighter, then ran his hands down the back of my jogging pants to my bare ass. I didn't have panties on. Knowing what was coming next, I inhaled lightly and prepared for the good sensation I knew was about to happen. Jayvon slid his fingertip up and down the crack of my ass, making me almost cream. I wasn't a stranger to anal action. I actually loved it. He tapped on the walls of my vagina, which were already wet and slippery. I lost my mind and squealed. The MacBook was a great gesture toward getting me to forgive him, but his touch sealed the deal.

Walking me back to the bed, he pushed me back and fell on top of me. I wrapped my legs tighter around him so he couldn't get up if he wanted to. He'd made his moves. It was time for me to take control and make a few. First, I stuck my tongue down his throat and passionately kissed him. Then I spread my legs wider and pushed my coochie up on him so he'd know the pressure was building up to explode.

"Oh, you want some of this dick? You gonna forgive ya manz?" He gripped my thighs and dragged me to the edge of the bed.

"Aah, yes, yeah, yup, I'll forgive you," I gave in, panting in between each word.

"Are you sure?" He teased me, applying more pressure to my clitoris.

I squirmed underneath his weight. "Quit playing. You know I want you. I need you—*all* of you."

Before I could tell him to lick me, he stuck it in and had me humming with one stroke.

"Uuuum, damn, you feel good as hell." All types of nasty shit were falling off my tongue.

"Shut up and take this dick," he growled.

Out of all his commands, I didn't mind following that one. Biting my lip, I arched my back and thrust my pussy toward his dick each time he pushed his meatiness into me. We were both panting, moaning, sweating, and grabbing on each other while we fucked, but neither of us spoke a word. It wasn't until my nut was nearing that I broke out uttering words.

"I love you. I love you. I love you. I love youuuu!" I dug my nails into his back and let the orgasm overtake me.

"Aw, naw, shorty-ma . . . I feel you tensin' up on a nigga, but it ain't time to bust a nut yet. I'm about to play up in this juicy pussy for hours," he smirked, slowed up his stroke, then pulled his wood up outta me without warning.

My pussy farted, and my body jerked a few times as I curled my lips into a pout and grasped for his chest. "Hmmm, you ain't right," I hissed, speaking on how he'd brought up my husband *and* teasing my needy anatomy.

Amp's cocky laugh filled the room. "C'mon, now, girl. Don't play ya mans like that. You know er' muthafuckin' thang about me is right." He slapped his meat against my thigh, then slid it up the opening of my coochie without letting it dip back in. It felt like my lips were vibrating and about to suck his meaty ass ten inches into my soul.

Amp's ego was bigger than his manhood was, but I couldn't blame him. I was codependent as hell on this man, no matter how much I tried fighting against it.

"I love the fuck out of you, baby." He put his hands around my neck, then kissed me intensely.

The mixture of pleasure and pain started sending me over the edge. Jayvon sucked from my nipples up to my neck and lips and then back down to the part of me that was lusting for his touch the most. I was quivering, damn near chewing a hole in my lip, and gasping for air each time he tugged and sucked on my clitoris.

The room spun. I think I saw stars, and I swear to God I felt my toes tingle from the touch of his tongue. My entire body felt warm from the inside out. He was scribbling his name into my pussy repeatedly as I held his head in place with one hand while gripping the sheet with my other. My cuticles were on fire from me trying to stay still. I ain't give a fuck what he thought about me once I climbed up out of his bed at this point 'cause I was chasing my nut.

I used the heel of my foot to hold him in place as he applied pressure to my G-spot. He was eager to please, and that was something I'd been missing. With me being so busy with school, our sex life had been on some hit-and-quit-it, get-ya-nut-quick type shit.

I went wild when he stuck his thumb into my booty hole. Amp had me trying all types of freaky shit. I was at his mercy and lovin' it. "Please don't stop."

"Shut the fuck up, girl. You ain't gotta tell me how to handle no pussy." The rougher he got, the more I got off.

This session between us wasn't about making love and catching feelings, but straight fuckin' makeup sex. Plus, I had to make him remember exactly what he had at home. I was about to come hard for this nigga. So. Damn. Hard. My shrieks poured out into the room. Fuck being modest. I wanted every single inch of him stroking me to ecstasy. I couldn't stop humming as my cat purred for him. My back was broken, my clit was swollen, and my body was going through a million different sexual spasms simultaneously.

"Yeah, shorty . . . I'm 'bout to stroke this li'l pussy out real good. I'ma have to apologize to you in advance for how dirty I'ma do you."

Before I could contest or take a deep breath, he threw my right leg over his shoulder and dug into my guts again. My voice was caught in my throat, and I damn near slid up the headboard, running from his dick. He stroked me like a straight savage, and I kept getting wetter.

"You gonna have a nigga's baby, girl," he grunted, then unloaded in me, not knowing I was secretly on birth control and popped it this morning on time like clockwork. I'd gladly get off them once he moved us out of the hood, but till then, I was blocking all the babies he tried shooting up in me.

Jayvon was still collapsed across the bed, trying to catch his breath when I peeled myself off the sticky sheets and entered the kitchen. Cum was dripping from out of me, and my knees were wobbly. He'd dug me to the point of my vagina being raw, yet I was still floating on cloud nine. Now that Jayvon was on board with me being in school, I felt like the sky could be the limit for us.

Feeling close to dehydrated, I filled a glass of tap water and grabbed Jayvon a beer from the fridge. The coldness of the can felt good against my warm skin. After soaping a warm washcloth, I returned to the bedroom, where Jayvon stroked his manhood back up.

"Climb ya ass back in this bed for round two," he commanded.

"You ain't ready." I walked over to the bed seductively.

Gently tugging me down by my hair, I fell on top of him and his hard dick. "You feel that monster, ma? Do something about it."

Jayvon and I fucked around until sunset. He was lightly snoring, and I was lying still, listening to the sounds of the hood pouring into my raised window. All the kids outside riding bikes, playing tag, and relay racing were replaced by their gossiping parents. Now, all I heard outside my window was fiends calling up and down the street for one another, stray dogs howling, and a bunch of common folk chattering about pointless shit. Sleep was for folks with jobs or somewhere to be in the morning. My neighbors weren't part of that population.

Jayvon shifted and woke up, pulling my attention from my thoughts, so I pushed my booty back up on him. "Nah, babe. You see what time it is. I'ma have to finish breaking you off after we make sure the trap houses are straight." Stretching and yawning, he climbed out of bed right into his stone-washed jeans.

I didn't budge and wasn't planning to until I got my way. Since Jayvon was playing make-up to me anyway, I figured getting him to compromise shouldn't be that hard. "The only way you're leaving this house is if you promise to take me on a date. We can trap after the date or before. I'll let you pick that part."

Sighing while shaking his head, he pulled the cover off me and told me to get up. "Get dressed with ya wannabe shot-callin' ass. Got a nigga jumping in circles and shit."

"Nope, more like chasing ya tail in circles. That's what dogs do." Winking and smirking, I kissed his frowned lips. "I'll be dressed in a few. After you take me on a date to my favorite steakhouse and give me another dose of dick, I might forgive you."

Chapter 15

Jayvon

Morgan laid across my chest, stroking my dick and watching Netflix was how our evening was playing out. Times like this were what I'd been missing with shorty. Since she started being scholarly, I hadn't been cooped up in the house caking.

This afternoon after we finally woke up, I went to her boutique and did a few light repairs and chores while she did inventory and some other odds and ends. Collecting from the trap was the last thing we did, and I'd made that a pickup and drive-off mission, having Dex bring the bag to the curb on some hot shit. Tonight, though, I was supposed to meet up with the fellas for a tournament of Madden. Hopefully, Morgan wouldn't be tripping about me busting up since I'd been catering to her every desire. Last night, I'd done it up for shorty on some shit she called romantic.

We dined at a restaurant off the water, where I had them serve us the best bottle of wine and her a big-ass piece of strawberry cheesecake (her favorite). It wasn't on my to-do list, but we took a horse and carriage ride through downtown Detroit on some new hipster shit movement the city was undergoing. When I was growing up, muthafuckas would've shot and killed a horse in Detroit for the hair to wear as weave and not ride them.

White people moved in, and, *pow,* we're diversifying and shit. It wasn't no thang to me, especially since Morgan was impressed enough to be all over me. Then we ended the night sitting and talking by the water.

Morgan had been in my ear tough about changing up my pace, how I hustled, and how we lived on a daily basis. But last night, she made a nigga realize how selfish I'd been in making her struggle. She came down to my level, upgraded me, and loved me wholeheartedly the entire time. I knew I needed to run her down the aisle sooner than later. She deserved a badass ring and a wedding on an island or some romantic shit like that.

"Bae, after the movie goes off, I've really gotta hit the books and study for a little while." She looked up at me with puppy dog eyes. "Don't be mad because, after a couple of hours, you'll be glad we didn't argue now."

"You good, bae. I'ma be up front counting up. Holla if you need a nigga for a distraction." I leaned over and kissed her stomach. "Damn, I can't wait to put my seed up in you."

She blushed. "Get out to that living room, Jayvon. You ain't ready to be a daddy, for real."

"I'ma show you all of what a nigga ready for. Just give a nigga a li'l more time."

Turning up the sounds of my favorite street rapper, I was deep in the zone. I stayed bumping rap whenever I was in grande mode. All the money we'd collected was spread across the table, getting tallied up, bill by bill. Me and mine were eating good off the li'l operation Morgan truly engineered. Her feisty ass was a genius. Although I kept dangling my dick around other bitches, I'd kill any of them hoes for my Lia. She was worthy of owning the world in my eyes.

Knocks at the door took me off my square, making me slide my pistol from underneath the couch cushion—on ready. People didn't just pop up at my crib.

"Helloooo, Jayvon, it's your mother. Let me in. It's pouring down rain like crazy out here," Valerie shouted from the other side of my door.

"Damn," I whispered, hurrying to stuff the money back into the duffle bags.

I knew my momma was over here looking for a few dollars for her nightcap. She stayed with her hand out like I was the ATM. She wanted her share of my profits since she'd introduced me to the streets, then allowed me to drop out of high school to slang. On some hood shit, it's like she wanted to be my manager with a guaranteed percentage of my street game. My momma stayed coming for mine. Tossing the bags into the front closet, I opened the door to a still-screaming Valerie.

Morgan

After taking a long shower, I lit a blunt, then curled up on the bed with my laptop. The last couple of days cuddled up with Jayvon had been great, but it was time to buckle down. Bryce sent some more notes and a study guide via email he'd put together himself to help me out. In return for him looking out, I'd used my hookup with a few distributors and ordered him some slacks and Ralph Lauren button-ups for the low. They'd get delivered to the boutique, so Jayvon wouldn't catch me and question me. It was strange as hell trying to shop for Bryce because I was so used to shopping for my thuggish man, so hopefully, Bryce would like my versions of his style.

When I heard Jayvon turn the stereo on blast, I knew he was about to be in the zone, counting up for a good minute. That shit was like a hobby for him. I pulled out my phone and called Bryce. I needed him to give me a pep talk and explain some of the concepts that were stumping me. Sliding a towel up to the crack beneath the door would help me hurry off the phone with Bryce if Jayvon came in, and I could tell Jayvon it was to help muffle the noise since I was studying.

Bryce answered on the fourth ring. "Hey, Morgan. Nice to hear from you. To what do I owe the pleasure of your phone call tonight?" He sounded so proper.

I sighed. "I'm over here struggling, which has become the only tune I've been singing lately. Did I catch you at a bad time, or can you help me?"

"When it comes to you, there's never a bad time. Of course I can help you."

"I've already got a surprise for you. You're gonna make me double up on it by being extra nice and supportive. I swear I would've dropped this class by now if it wasn't for you."

"You don't have to get me anything for helping you out, Morgan. I do it because I want to. However, I'ma take your gift." He laughed. "You can bring it over now if you want to." I heard him flirting and dropping innuendos.

I wasn't offended, nor did I take him seriously. It was Bryce talking. He was always a gentleman, respectful and kind. When he picked up on my silence because I really didn't know how to respond or what to say, he continued over his comment on to what I'd called about.

We went through each bullet point I'd highlighted that was causing concern for me. Bryce took his time trying to make sure he broke the lesson down just like the professor had done, so I tried my hardest not to make him repeat himself and took my own notes for extra clarification later.

By the time we were done, I was a little more confident about taking the final. The only thing that worried me was whether I could retain all the information over a few days. It was going to take way more hours of studying. Although I didn't want Bryce to think I was only using him, I rushed off the phone, yawning and playing like I was exhausted and kinda stressed because I heard the music turn off. I wasn't trying to get caught by Jayvon looking suspicious with my li'l creep study session over with.

"I really appreciate you pumping my brain up with so much knowledge, but now I'm exhausted." I told a corny joke to butter him up. "I'll see you in the morning."

"It'll be a good morning. See you then." He was corny with me right back, then hung up before I did.

Jayvon

"What in the hell was you doing up in here that you had me on the porch in the rain for so long? I'm ya damn momma, boy. You better show me some respect." She was talking smack, forgetting how shit played out the last time we saw each other. "When you came to my house the other day at the crack of ass, I didn't leave you on the porch."

"Chill out, Ma. I came as soon as I heard you yelling. I wasn't doing shit but burning this backwoods and listening to some gangster music." I divulged half the truth, wanting her to be quiet before Morgan heard I'd left the house the other night without her knowing.

She smacked her lips, looking at me like she didn't believe a word that left my mouth. I ain't never been able to pull no wool over Valerie's eyes—not as a child or an adult. Fear wasn't something I had for niggas in the street, but it wasn't a strange emotion when it came to her. My moms always put her foot off into my ass and would probably do it today.

"Pass that blunt and quit lying to me, Jayvon. I raised yo' ass, so I can sense when you're feeding me bullshit," she called me out.

"Whatever, Ma. Take this blunt and chill out before you get to going. That shit hitting hard as a motha—"

She snatched the blunt from my hand and hit it like she was trying to burn the whole wrap. Then she blew out a fourth of it in a circle, quickly sucking it all back in. Two seconds later, she started choking till tears gathered in her eyes. That's when you knew the shit was good . . . so good that you had to hit it again. Valerie did. My mom was the one who'd taught me how to smoke, so I knew she wasn't playing about tasting every last crystal on the green buds. I got my MaryJane addiction from her.

"You're right, son. This is some fire. Throw Momma a couple of these kind of baggies along with a few of them dollars you collected earlier. I know you holding. Don't leave ya momma hanging." Waltzing to the couch, she sat down and kicked her feet up on the table.

I went in my pocket and peeled off a few dollars she could have. I wasn't about to open the front closet to me and Morgan's stash. Valerie would've had a field day going for mine.

"Okay, so enough of the bullshit. Have you heard from Jinx? What's the word on that issue?"

"It's not a word to tell you. That nigga been incognito since he popped up out of thin air. He hasn't shown his face or called me about any work. Nor could me and Raj put eyes on him when we rode through his stomping grounds the other day."

Shaking her head, Valerie walked to the window and peeked out the blinds. "Just like you were groomed for the streets, he was too. Make sure you stay prepared, strapped with an extra clip."

The whole conversation between me and my moms ended with hearing Morgan's footsteps. Morgan not knowing who Jinx was and that I killed his father, would stay that way. From the day my mom put the setup into motion, we vowed to take the secret to our graves.

My thoughts about Jinx and Spencer were pushed to the back of my mind when Morgan finally entered the room. Her face was ripped with disgust. I knew there was about to be friction before a word was spoken simply because the two I loved didn't get along. Plus, the argument from the other night hadn't made their relationship better.

It was hard for me to pick my family over my girlfriend because I'd given Morgan the ammunition she needed to feel some type of way about Valerie. I told her everything about my childhood and how Valerie used me to get cash for herself. To be honest, the only reason I hadn't cut ties with my mother was because I'd only get one. She'd have to pay for how she treated me with whatever God she prayed to when her time came. Until then, I was gonna keep holding her down.

Anyhow, my moms got a bad taste in her mouth behind Morgan the first time she laid eyes on her. She said my boo was uppity and only wanted some thuglike dick 'cause all the preppy boys she'd probably had access to all her life wasn't fucking like a hood boy. She didn't welcome Morgan as my girlfriend back in the day and not as my girlfriend now.

"Uh-uh, you're gonna have to take your feet up off my furniture, Momma Valerie," Morgan sassed on purpose, finding something smart to say.

Looking at Morgan with her nose flared, my mother responded smartly while getting more comfortable with her feet on our coffee table. "You wouldn't even have none of this nice stuff if it wasn't for my son. *You* moved in with *him,* remember?"

"I don't have to because you remember enough for both of us."

Valerie took Morgan's not saying much back as a sign of her giving up the argument and decided to twist an already-stabbed knife. "I bet your parents remember too." Once the last word was spoken, my mother looked satisfied.

She'd intentionally gunned to get underneath Morgan's skin, and it worked. Morgan might've been a tough girl, a hitta, and my ride or die, but she had a soft spot for her parents. She grew up like her last name was Huxtable, but they'd disowned her because of her choice to love me. Although she didn't talk about it much, I knew she missed them and wished they'd forgive her. Low-key, I think that's why she was trying so hard to get her degree—so they'd approve of her. Morgan gave up her foundation for me. The least I could do was check my ill-mannered-ass momma. "Yo, Ma, here's those baggies yo' ass asked for. Rise on up and go back down the street to your crib. Like I told you before, don't be coming down here trying to stir up no bullshit. We all might need a couple of hours apart."

"They've got a special place in hell for little boys who don't respect the woman who birthed 'em." Uncrossing her feet off the table, she stood up and matched the grim stare Morgan was cutting into her with. "I ain't scared of you, little girl, so you can quit barking up this tree for an old-school beat down."

Morgan smacked her lips, rolled her eyes, and then looked over at me to reinforce what I'd already said. So I did. "Ma, I don't know how to say chill in another language, but bring it down and quit gunning for my girl, first of all. Secondly, I ain't no little boy. I'm a grown-ass man. And if I'm gonna go to hell, it's gonna be because of all the gritty shit I do in the streets. Remember that."

Snatching the bags of weed from the palm of my hand, she couldn't leave without having the last word. "I can't believe you're putting me back out in the rain for this little heifer. The pussy must be like dynamite—*Boom!*" Valerie was being dramatic.

"Quit dissing me, Momma Valerie. Jayvon's hand is not the only hand that feeds you." This time, it was Morgan gunning to get a reaction.

Right as I opened my mouth to try breaking up their argument again, my mother's hand flew up to shush me. "Naw, son, it's too late for you to say anything on my behalf now. You should've never brought this bird home or let her think she'd ever be hardcore enough to bump heads with a seasoned bitch." Valerie entered my house with the first word and left it with the last word.

"I swear to God, I can't stand your momma. She's disrespectful as hell, Jayvon. I'm tired of her coming and going like she pleases, and I want that shit to stop. She's got a house you pay all the damn bills on. She can stay at it."

I didn't feel like arguing about her and my mother tonight. Their animosity for each other hadn't done anything but grown over the nine years of them being acquainted, so I knew nothing was about to change. "I'm gonna handle what I can, baby. But in the meantime, be cool and quit antagonizing her. You already know how my moms is."

"That ain't no damn excuse, Jayvon. I knew how my parents were and still went against the grain. Quit expecting me to keep taking the bullshit your mother dishes out. That's your mom, so she shouldn't have shit to say to me," she huffed. Although she was yelling and screaming, her words were filled with pain. When I looked into her eyes, they were filled with tears. "I can't believe I gave up my family just for you not to make me yours."

"Aww, come here, girl. I swear it ain't like that. I know your sacrifice for me, so I'm gonna make sure you know how much I appreciate it." Embracing her, I held Morgan while she cried. This wasn't something she did much, so I knew the pain was heavy.

Morgan let her tears soak my shirt for a few minutes before she pushed me up off her. "A'ight, I'm good. I just wanna get things back to normal with us and everything involving us." She sighed, seeming like her mind was elsewhere. "I'ma just call it a night and get some rest. I've got class and a sale at the boutique afterward tomorrow. I'll see you when you come to bed."

"A'ight. I'll be in there as soon as I finish counting up, baby. And on the real, don't doubt ya nigga. I got you. A nigga ain't bring you this far to not keep going."

She closed the door right after saying good night, never responding to my statement. It used to be on my heart that I held the key to Morgan's, but on the real, I felt my shorty slipping away. The next gift she got from me would be my last name.

Chapter 16

Morgan

"Morgan, babe, wake up," Jayvon whispered in my ear.

Waking up, it took me a moment to gather myself. I'd fallen asleep studying. My books were still around me. I knew it was two something in the morning because the rerun of the news was on that I'd watched at ten.

"Hey," I groggily glanced at the clock. "What were you doing that took you so long to come to bed?"

"Nothing. In the man cave on the sticks."

"Well, maybe I'll whoop off into your ass after my exam on Saturday," I said through a yawn.

One of the pastimes Jayvon and I shared back before things got heavy with our trap houses was playing video games. I actually missed those simple days. We'd sit on the couch for hours, blowing through blunt after blunt and shooting villains on *Black Ops*. Deep down in my heart, I really felt we still had a chance to be married and have a family if we could get back to enjoying each other. His next comment made me think he was in my mind.

With his arm resting on my stomach, he looked at me with puppy dog eyes. "I miss how we used to be, Mooka. I miss how you used to be all into me and only me. Damn, I wish we could get back to that."

Yeah, this nigga was buzzing for real. Jayvon only got overly emotional when he'd been drinking and smoking.

I had to watch what I said and how I said it from now on. His emotions were sometimes uncontrollable.

"I'm still right here, baby," I softly replied. "And I'm just as into you as I was on our first day of Chemistry class. It's always gonna be Morgan and Jayvon." I tried sounding convincing. As the words slipped from my lips, I wasn't sure if I meant them. It wasn't that I didn't love Jayvon 'cause the whole world knew I did. I just wasn't sure our relationship would genuinely stand the test of time.

"It better be us versus everybody forever, li'l momma. I know I've been fucking up a lot lately and giving you a hard time about school and shit, but a nigga love you. Real talk. I love your dirty drawers, Lia. That's my ma'fuckin word, and I put that on my life."

They say a drunk tongue speaks an honest truth. If that's so in all cases, my heart should've been lighting up with Jayvon's confession. He was pouring out his love and devotion to me. Although I wanted to wrap my arms around his neck and pull him in for a long kiss, I couldn't match his emotion.

"Come on, Jayvon. Let's go to bed," I sighed, trying to roll over.

Jayvon held his weight down on me so I couldn't move. "Naw, not until you tell me how much you love me back and that you're still gonna hold a nigga down after you get your degree or whatever."

I knew not to answer differently, even if there was a slight chance that I didn't feel how he wanted me to feel. "You shouldn't be worried about me holding you down, Jayvon. I'm the one who's been waiting around for years to get wifed." I thought bringing up marriage would send him running to bed, but he fed into my comment.

"Do you really wanna marry a nigga, Mooka? Just as I am?"

"I'm not trying to argue with you, so let's not go down that road, Jayvon. You know I love you, but I'm not sure you're ready to settle down. Let's keep it one hundred."

Jayvon looked like he was giving my words some thought. "Give a nigga some time, and I swear, I'ma give you that." Cuddling up to me, Jayvon rested his face into my neck and fell asleep.

Chapter 17

Officer Keidan

"You've been spending a lot of man hours on this case, Keidan. Have you made enough progress for us to start closing in?" I was in my sergeant's office, debriefing.

"Not just yet, but I'm very close to making a breakthrough. I've got someone on the inside now."

"Very close is not going to get me off your back. I need more than that. They're coming down hard on me, so I'm coming down hard on you. Give me something to keep this case going, or I'm shutting it down now," he barked.

"Sir, please, with all due respect, if they start pushing in on this case—on any of the pawns—it can throw the entire case off." I started breaking the case down to him, all the moving parts and how they were all connected. "The more I investigate, the more I find. This is the big one."

"Look, this is what I will give you, Keidan—one week. You've got one week to get this worked out and closed. I want the folder on my desk with the details in less than that. Like I told you, people are breathing down my throat over this case, and I don't want them sending another damn department lead over here to micromanage how I manage. I won't have you fucking up my peace."

"I understand. I got you."

"You better do more than that." He waved me out of his office. "Don't sleep until this shit is done."

I left my boss's office and returned to my think tank to spread out all the pieces I'd collected during the past few months on this case. I'd been busting my ass trying to bring this organization down, and it finally started to feel like that might happen.

I laid out pictures, told a story with the evidence, then put in order who I would pull in for questioning. I had to be strategic so the case wouldn't fall apart. I knew they'd talk to start collaborating once the first person got interrogated.

"I need you down here," I called my informant.

"Aye, man, it's hot right now. I can't just be popping up at a police station."

"You can, and you better if you don't wanna go to jail. I'll pick your punk ass up right now," I threatened.

"A'ight, man, chill. Give me a few to make sure ain't nobody on me."

"Don't fuck with me, or I *will* find you," I warned.

When I'd first started working on this case, it was a trickle-down from a task force the city had to cut down on crime and drug trafficking within the flagged areas of the city. They wanted the drugs off the streets, the pushers in prison, and the property they were consuming wiped out so housing could be developed. The new mayor was trying to build up the city of Detroit, which I respected. So much so that I'd thrown myself head-on into the case, undercover, to collect as much information on Amp, one of the biggest drug dealers in the city, and his entire organization down to his mama were looking at indictments.

Chapter 18

Morgan

Sipping from a hot cup of coffee I'd gotten from Starbucks, I was reading over my notes for like the hundredth time since the last class meeting. I hated not being able to follow Professor Harris when she lectured, so I was trying to do everything possible to prevent that. I'd studied the notes I'd taken, the ones Bryce emailed, the chapters in the book, and even some reading material on the internet after the argument with Jayvon. Actually, the fight ended up fueling me to study harder.

I'd gotten out of bed as soon as the sun broke through a night of having sex repeatedly, leaving Jayvon wrapped up in the sheets. His waking me up in the middle of my sleep ruined all the rest I'd gotten, but he'd made it worth it. The last time I was in class, we were in a bad spot. We got half of Saturday, then all of Sunday to get it right before today, but his mom fucked up our Sunday night. I was pushing all that down because, at the end of the day, I had to walk before I could run or fly.

My phone rang, breaking my concentration.

"Ha! Ain't this a trip," I said under my breath, looking at my phone's screen. It was Nakeya calling. Since Friday, we still hadn't spoken.

I answered, but she started talking before I got to say a word. "I'm already cranking orders out at the boutique for a few of my day shift girls, but Jos isn't here yet. Do you want me to make these sales or no?" She said all that with attitude, not even saying hello first.

"Um, don't you think you should address the two-day hiatus *you* were just on?" I gave her an equal amount of attitude.

She smacked her lips. "Not really. I mean, it is what it is. You're always the first one screaming 'be about your brand' and 'carry yourself like a professional', but popped off, ruining my event. Had it been an exclusive party for this boutique, you wouldn't have dared to trip on Jayvon like that. It's cool, though. You're spoiled and condescending. I see how it is."

Swallowing my pride and admitting I was wrong was effortless. Nakeya was 1,000 percent right. At the end of the day, I didn't want us at odds or bitter with each other. Real friends don't have to walk around with baggage that weighs down their relationship. We're supposed to stay lifting up each other.

"My bad. It ain't shit I can say, but I'm sorry. Besides the liquor, I got caught in my feelings and should've been focused on you and what you've got popping—just like you support me day in and out. Are we good? Do you accept my apology?"

"Yeah, girl, we're good." She sounded kinda dry, but I figured that meant she simply needed a few more days to get over it.

"Okay, but about taking those orders, hell yeah, make that money. Thanks for looking out."

"Yup-yup. See you when you get here."

As soon as I hung up the phone, I turned off the ringer to avoid a repeat confrontation with the professor.

Hearing Bryce's voice, I turned around to see him and some random bland classmate of ours entering the lecture hall, conversing and laughing. I don't know why, but I was looking forward to seeing him, and the first sight of him with another girl irked me. Chalking it up to just being appreciative of the good conversation we shared and how much he helped me stay afloat thus far in class, I ignored the fluttering butterflies in my stomach and walked over to him.

"Good morning, Bryce," I greeted him but ignored the female he was talking to him. It wasn't anything personal. I just don't mingle with different chicks outside my clique.

She sucked her teeth but not loud enough to irk me and then excused herself a few spaces down to her seat. We didn't have assigned places to sit but usually kept it consistent from week to week. Bryce noticed the pettiness and lightly chuckled.

"Women. I swear I'll never understand y'all for as long as I live."

"Don't feel bad. Every man on God's green earth will die not knowing how females' brains work," I joked.

"The sad thing is that you're probably right," he agreed and laughed along with me. "But anyway, good morning, right back at ya. It's nice to see a smile on your face."

I smiled even wider. "Thanks. I'm trying to start this day off on a positive note."

"That plan almost flew out the window a few minutes ago with ol' girl, but okay," he responded sarcastically.

I smacked my lips, then playfully rolled my eyes. "Quit playing and take this cup of coffee as a thank you for helping me out with the notes."

"Thanks, but the only reason I'm taking this is because I could use the caffeine after the long night I had. You'll never owe me for something I've done for you. I keep telling you that."

"Yeah, but I'm not the type of chick who takes handouts. Please accept this small gesture, at least."

"Done. Now g'on and get ready for class. Holla at me at break time if you need some help making sense of the notes. I already went through the chapters ahead of time." Taking a big gulp of the cooled-down coffee he could've had piping hot if he'd been here thirty minutes ago like I was.

"Damn, yo' ass is a nerd. I can barely keep up, and you've already skipped ahead."

"Yup, yup, and you keep coming to my nerdy ass." He grinned and winked. "And just for that smart remark, I'll take a coffee every time you stop at Starbucks before class."

"I'm gonna get me another Steve Urkel," I joked, spun around, and walked away.

"Keep talking, and your broke-down Sheryl Underwood ass is gonna be getting me bagels and Dunkin' Donuts too. You ain't funny, Morgan."

I didn't turn around or respond to him, but I laughed all the way to my seat. My face felt hot and flushed. Bryce made me act like I used to back as a schoolgirl when I was too shy to talk to boys. Anyhow, I got back to my front and center seat just in time.

"Good morning, class. I hope you slept well because you'll have to retain a lot of information today. Who can tell me about asset turnover?"

A hush was over the class. I looked back at Bryce. He smirked at me, then gave Professor Harris her answer. When I mouthed "nerd" at him again, he held up the cup of coffee and mouthed the word "bagel."

I might've been hee-hee-ha-ha-ing with him on the outside, but I was sighing on the inside. I should've thought ahead of the game and read the chapters listed on the syllabus for this week too. My phone lit up on my desk with a message from Jayvon saying he loved me and to have a good day in class. Although I was happy he was showing support, I ignored it and started copying the diagrams from the PowerPoint spreadsheet.

Professor Harris hadn't held us up. My fingers were burning from how fast I had to write to keep up with how quickly she talked. I peeked over at Bryce to see if he was keeping up so I could get the notes, and even he was trying to keep up but still participating in the lecture. I swear he made shit seem so easy. Regardless of whether I wanted to, I would have to take him up on his offer to tutor me. That's the only way I saw myself passing the class.

During the break, I stayed behind and got extra time with the professor on things I didn't understand. She was more than helpful and happy to see all the effort I'd put in since the last time we'd spoken. When I felt like it was the perfect time, I told her how a few of her suggestions worked for me with the boutique. It might've seemed like I was kissing her ass—and that's because I was. You see, I understood the concept of doing what you have to do to survive.

Jayvon

Morgan had gone to class, Marva was cleaning the house, and Popps was outside mowing the lawn. It was always boring around the house without my woman. We used to sit in bed eating bowls of cereal and watching cartoons like little kids before she started school. Now, it's like she didn't have time for a nigga. I almost did some cake shit, like cuddling up with her pillow and reminiscing on how she was throwing that ass back on me, trying to match me for each stroke I was giving her ass last night, but I chose to man up. It was times like this I knew I didn't need to be out there creeping and cheating 'cause shorty had my heart wrapped up.

Rolling out of bed, I slid on my Nike flops and made my way to the kitchen for a protein shake. I thought about making a solo ride to the West or even calling Raj to see if he wanted to ride shotgun to go looking for Jinx but decided against it. If and when ol' boy got at me, I was gonna be strapped and ready.

After looking outside and surveying what was popping with the neighbors, I went into the basement and cranked my stereo up on some of Pac's rhymes so I could get a few reps in. Not a day passed that didn't involve me exercising, toning up, and building my muscle mass. I had to stay ready for these niggas. I did push-ups, chin-ups, bench-pressed some weights, and got a good sweat in from boxing the weighted bag. Working out was a good way to clear my mind and refill it with my agenda for the day.

Part of our basement was set up like a gym and even included a treadmill, stair stepper, and a wall of mirrors she used to work on her glutes while admiring herself. There were even two 32-inch flat-screen televisions mounted to the wall so we could both watch our shows individually while working out together. And, of course, they were set up to work with our Bluetooth headsets, so we didn't have to disturb each other while together.

I ain't really wanna admit it, but I kinda missed her hawking my moves and being around. She was switching up the dynamic I'd gotten accustomed to.

"Excuse me, boss. I'm done cleaning the house. Is there anything else you'd like me to do?" Marva shouted down the steps at me.

"Naw, naw, you're good, Marva. I'm on my way up so I can pay you." Hitting the top of the stairs, I walked into a pristine kitchen that smelled of Clorox and Palmolive dish detergent. The floor was spotless, all the dishes had been washed, dried, and put up, and the walls were slightly damp where Marva had wiped them down.

"I also cleaned out the refrigerator and cabinets, boss." Marva noticed me checking out her work. "Do you want me to make a store run?"

"Morgan might call you later, but I'm good," I responded, handing over fifty dollars—two crumbled-up twenties and two five-dollar bills.

"Okay," she sang, happily snatching the money from my fingertips. "Thanks so much. I'm about to be out. You already know what I'm about to get off into."

Marva hurried out of the house so she could get high. The only thing she was about to do was to spend my money at the trap, which meant giving it right back to me. I'd already dropped a few dollars in Popps' pocket earlier, and the lawn was neatly mowed, so I knew he was cooped up and getting high. If either one of them could kick their nasty drug habits I help them nurture, they'd be beneficial to their families . . . or at least themselves.

My cell phone vibrated in my hand.

Looking down at the screen of my phone, I thought twice about answering because the number wasn't programmed and was coming up unknown. The only reason I answered was because of Jinx. I wanted it to be him. I wanted him to make good on his word of getting at me—so I could get at him.

"Yo, who 'dis?" I answered, hearing nothing but loud music and girls giggling in the background. "Yo, yo, who 'dis?" I asked again, louder than I had the first time.

"'Sup, Jayvon? Hold on a sec. My bad," the dude said, then yelled into his background. "Ay, pipe y'all cum-thirsty asses down before y'all get some more nut squirted down ya throats to gag ya quiet." A few seconds later, Barz was back on the line addressing me. "Yeah, like I said, Jayvon, that's my bad. I ain't been able to spit a fire track all day for these hoes actin' up."

"The industry's got their hands full with yo' nutty ass, Barz, man. But what else is up? What's good?"

"Nothin' much but the same thang. I was trying to see if you could hook me up with shorty from the other night. She was hittin' like a muthafucka." He was talking in code about wanting some more of the weight I'd sold him.

"Fa'sho. That ain't no thang. You whippin' through the hood in that Beamer to pick her up from over here, or you want me to drop shorty off? She ain't got no whip to meet you." I kept the front up.

"It'll be sweet if you can drop her off this way. I'll throw you some gas money."

"Naw, B. You know me better than that, so don't play me short. I ain't broke, and I ain't never got my hand out on no petty shit like gas."

"Dog, be chill. I know ya pedigree fa'sho, but play ya position 'cause I ain't mean you no disrespect." Barz took a cop but put me in check at the same time. He wasn't belittling me because he'd gotten on. He was still in character.

"My bad. Damn. A nigga stay in go mode. Plus, I got some other shit going on." I took my own cop. "But send me the address to where you want me to drop shorty off at, and I'm there. What time you trying to get at her?"

"The sooner, the better. I'll send that info over right now. Tell shorty to come extra prepared." I read that as code for bringing more than the last time.

"I got you. I'll let her know. See you in a few."

Off the line with Barz, I called Dex so he could get me together some weight. I didn't want to keep Mr. Celebrity waiting, and I'm saying that because his money was large. Loyal customers got loyal service. That's something Morgan taught me. With no hate or evil intent, I wanted Barz to keep rising to the top and buying dope from me each level of the way.

I hopped in the shower, washed my ass, then brushed my teeth. Morgan made sure Marva did weekly runs to the laundromat and dry cleaners, so it didn't take me but a second to jump sweet. I was about to meet Barz at the studio, so I couldn't do it on 'em no less. Hermès belt, Louboutin shoes, a cold 'fit, and a loaded heater concealed on my hip, I walked out of the house feeling clean and crisp, sorta untouchable.

Dex was walking to the curb when I pulled up in front of the trap. Getting in, he slid me the weight I'd requested first, then threw me dap and spoke. "Did you get my message about taking care of ol' boy?"

"Yeah, no doubt. I did, and I'm proud of you for moving so quickly and efficiently." First, giving him his earned praise, I now had to school him about the aftermath. "But now you've gotta make sure to keep your eyes and ears open at all times. Just because you killed that young nigga don't mean you're supposed to tilt ya cap and drop ya pistol. He's got family, homies, foes that might've wanted to reconcile, jumpoffs, maybe a baby momma, and some kids. Even a nobody has a somebody."

"So, what you're saying is that I should watch my back and quit boasting?"

"Yup, you've got it. That, plus I'ma have Raj sit over here and oversee thangs until I feel the smoke's settled. Once ol' boy's body is in the ground, his loved ones have mourned and forgotten about him, and any homies he had on his team have gotten whatever acts of revenge they wanna try out of their systems, we'll all go back to normal."

"So, is Raj the new muscle? I done put in work and get demoted?" Dex questioned, feeling slighted, though he was jumping the gun.

I chuckled, humored by his young ass. "Pipe down, li'l buddy. Poppin' off at the boss, better yet, the one who ordered you to kill, probably ain't the best idea. If I told you to kill, a life ain't shit to me. Feel me?"

Biting his lower lip, he nodded. "I got you."

"Good. Now that we're past that, let's get back to how business is gonna switch up until I say otherwise." After pausing for a few seconds to see if there was going to be a grunt, murmur, or movement of discomfort from Dex, I continued. "Think of Raj as your muscle more so than your overseer. Anything or anyone you have a problem with, he'll make sure it's not a problem. And anyone he has a problem with, I'll make sure he won't have that problem for long." It went without saying that Dex was included in the problems I'd eliminate if necessary. The tone of my voice was meant for him to read between the lines and fear me.

"Understood, and like always, I'ma handle mine and hold it down, boss."

"A'ight. G'on and get ya face right, then back to business."

Up the street and off the block, I called Raj, letting him know I was on the way.

Morgan

The lecture was over, but I wanted to get a few study hours in since I couldn't get a moment of peace at home. The pep talk with Professor Harris had my momentum on ten and me seeing the light at the end of the tunnel. With my textbook, notes, and handouts spread across a table in the student center, I looked up articles and supporting references for a paper we'd been assigned to write. The large percentage it was worth could shoot my grade up a whole letter—or down. Acing it was the outcome I really needed. After putting a dent in this project, I planned to type an outline I could quickly study throughout the day. I was trying to make the best of my second chance.

Buzz, buzz, buzz.

My cell vibrated across the table to Jayvon texting me.

Hubby: Hey, babe. U good?

I knew he was asking that because it was past the time I got out of school, and I hadn't checked in yet. Jayvon knew my schedule like the back of my hand, just like I knew his.

Me: Sorry I didn't call, bae. I'm good. I'm still at school rushing to get some stuff together for a paper I've gotta write. U good?

While waiting for him to reply, I continued with what I was doing so I could get to the boutique. The doors were already open for business and cranking dollars per Jos's check-in text.

Hubbs: Yup, yup, I'm 100. Do U. I'm 'bout to get in the streets.

"Do me? How am I supposed to take that? Please don't start with me, Jayvon," I blurted out. The two students studying at a nearby table looked at me rudely as if to say *be quiet*, but I shot them a return glare that said *mind your damn business*. Before I could respond to the text message, another one came in that settled my mood.

Hubbs: I love U.

Me: You better because I love you too. I'll call you when I leave here.

Hubbs: Make sure U do that. Two Up.

Placing my phone back on the table, I pulled my baseball cap brim farther down over my face and slumped down in my seat. It was only a few hours into my day, and already, my plate was running over with responsibilities. "Come on, Morgan. Get it together and let's crank out the rest of this work." I gave myself a pep talk.

"That's the type of spirit I like to hear."

I would've jumped from my seat, but Bryce held me down by the shoulders. He was oddly strong, though it didn't seem like he had that much muscle mass.

"I know you've been stressing about Professor Harris and the boutique, but you need to loosen up. You're tense as hell," he commented on my stress knots.

As he was massaging my shoulders, I could feel myself relaxing. His touch was comforting, soothing, and melting away my stress. Before I knew it, soft moans escaped my lips. "Wow, that feels amazing. Please, don't stop." Allowing my eyes to stay closed, I knew it was wrong to let this man close in my space, but it felt so good. Bryce might've looked like a lightweight, but he had some muscle behind him that had me seeing stars.

"You're with the wrong man if he's letting you walk around tense like this."

Leaning up so he'd get the point to take his hands off me, I spun around in my seat with questions. "I ain't never told you whether I had a boyfriend, so what's with the assumption?"

"Whoa, don't bite off my head. I just assumed you had a significant other because I heard a man yelling out for you while we were on the phone the other evening. Since you threw that word out there, I'd already 'assumed' it, but my apology if I'm wrong."

Rolling my eyes, I turned back around in the chair with a look of admittance on my face. I'd withheld divulging anything about my relationship status to Bryce, Professor Harris, and everyone linked to this school because I didn't want to answer questions about Jayvon. It was enough trying to balance a "good" and "bad" lifestyle along with a shitload of schoolwork. The last thing I needed to invest time in remembering was a boatload of lies to dress Jayvon and our way of life up to be accepted around here.

Now that I was being confronted head-on, I had to at least fess up that I indeed have a man. Besides, I was starting to feel unsure of my feelings toward Bryce. He was only supposed to be a cool and intelligent classmate I used to help me get by in school. But from how I started to feel around him, our connection was obviously growing into something more. I needed to tell him I had a man so he'd quit making advances . . . That way, I wouldn't have to make sense of liking a nerd.

Huffing, I responded, "There's no apology necessary. You're right. I do have a man." I left it at that, not wanting to go too deep into details.

"Oh, well, then, my initial statement was right. You're with the wrong man if he's letting you walk around tense like this. If you were my girl, the world wouldn't even get to you." He attempted to pull me back by my shoulders to continue the massage, but I yanked my arm away, then leaped up.

"Whoa, whoa, whoa. I think you've got me twisted, Bryce. I appreciate you looking out for me with the notes and shit, but we're nothing more than friends. If I led you to believe anything more than that was about to pop off between us, my bad," I explained and apologized, feeling like I needed to shut him down, though a tiny part of me didn't want to.

"Point heard and understood. It's not your bad if I read you wrong. I'ma fall back."

"Good. I've gotta go, so I'll catch up with ya." Gathering up my stuff, I kept my lips pursed like I was angry, but my chest was really full of anxiety. Bryce had me feelin' some type of way, and I didn't like it. Or at least I knew I was not supposed to like it, so I was fighting it off. Strutting away, I focused on not tripping over my feet. I knew he watched my every step until I disappeared out the door. And even that, I liked.

Getting to the car, the first thing I did was flip the visor down and then the mirror. I had to look myself in the eyes to tell myself to get it the hell together. Bryce wasn't my type; even if he was, I wasn't his. The Morgan he knew wasn't a trap queen. Finally, catching my breath and feeling like I had some control, I dug my blunt from the console so it would be at my fingertips to light once I hit the free highway.

Tap, tap. There were two soft taps on my window, then Bryce's voice. "Morgan."

After shouting out, my whole body jerked, then froze. Bryce sneaking up on me snatched the breath I'd just caught right back out of me. My lungs felt empty.

"My bad, I'm sorry. It seems like I keep messing up with you today, but can you roll the window down a second?"

Throwing my keys into the ignition, I started the car and turned the air on at the same time as I rolled down all the windows to keep from hyperventilating. I was feeling a lot of anxiety mixed with butterflies in the pit of my stomach, not only because Bryce snuck up on me but also because I was kinda blushing and couldn't conceal it.

"What can I do for you, Bryce?" I questioned, acting like my face was not turning red.

"Well, maybe we can do something for each other. You take me to that coffee spot you got my coffee from earlier, and I'll get you caught up on a few chapters that'll be on the test."

In my mind, I told him no, thank you. In my mind, I told him it wouldn't be a good idea. In my mind, I told the pretty boy to push on because he was lingering around a dangerous dope man's girl. But in reality, I told him I'd wait here for him to pull up, then he could follow me to the coffee shop. His offer of helping me get caught up for the upcoming exam was too good to pass up.

Chapter 19

Jayvon

The studio was rocking. Before Raj and I even walked into the private room, we saw strippers coming in and out in packs like they were on shifts at the bar. It took us a minute to get patted down and cleared through Barz's li'l entourage and security team, which was time I used to peep the scene just in case I needed to break up outta there in a rush or unexpectedly.

"Ay, man, you can't bring that big boy inside," one of the security guards said, trying to stand firm with his arms crossed.

"Then it seems we've got a problem, big fella, because neither me nor my homeboy are unstrapping, and that's the rule. Ya boss can meet me on the curb for business for all I give a fuck."

"Naw, you've got it misunderstood. Ain't no problem, and ain't gon' be no problem. You ain't gotta unstrap, but ya gotta get the fuck up outta here."

Quickly putting his hand on his heater and responding, Raj didn't care about going out the door and spraying bullets into whoever wanted to step in the way. That's part of why I brought him with me—besides me wanting him to stay my voice of reason in a room full of hoes. His advice had gotten me through a rough patch with Morgan, and now his quick temper and rage were about to get us in a shootout.

"Whoa, yo! SG, man, back down. Boss would fire yo' ass if he knew you were out here giving these men a hard time. You oughta be shaking them niggas' hands instead, ya stupid muthafucka." In the nick of time, a dude I kinda recalled from the strip club came out of the studio, stopping bullets from flying.

"Jayvon, my manz, and Raj, it's a firm rule that guns not be permitted on the property and fa'damn sho in the sessions, so you'll have to excuse SG here 'cause he's only doing his job." The man extended an explanation that didn't make my stance any different. "But, of course, Barz said to break the rule. We're good as long as y'all stay good. At the end of the day, it's not beneficial for either one of us to create problems."

"You're absolutely right. Respect gains respect. So as long as there's no breaking of that rule, we'll stay good."

Walking into the studio session, I caught eyes with Barz first. Throwing his hand up and shaking his head as an apology, he waved me in. He was in the booth laying a track down with a girl on her knees in front of him. He was spitting about some shit he ain't never did in the hood: hustle and bang, but it sounded real and sellable. His flow was impeccable, not even with a gasp or stutter, though I saw shorty's head bobbing back and forth like she was gone off a few lines.

Matter of fact, the few girls that were scattered throughout the studio seemed too faded off coke, pills, or maybe the sizzy that was all over the room. And it was apparent they were gettin' trains run on 'em because it was only maybe but five or six of them but probably twenty niggas—not including Raj and me. This joint looked like a gritty-ass trap house where some sketchiness had the potential to unfold.

Raj grabbed a beer, cracked the top off with his teeth, then held the wall beside me. "Yeah, these Hollywood muthafuckas is wild, fa'sho. I like a gutter party, but I'm not sure I can fade even this." Having been off pills since a kid, Raj didn't even put an over-the-counter Motrin in his mouth.

"You ain't even lied. I'ma make this money fa'sho, but it don't look like this fella need a lick more of this girlie-girl."

Sitting back, waiting on Barz to finish putting a few verses down, we witnessed the assumption come true. One of the girls lay on her back and welcomed another girl on top of her mouth, while spreading her legs for one of the dudes. Then the chick getting her pussy eaten opened her mouth to suck dick while that nasty muthafucka spread his legs to get his ass fucked by another dude.

I lost my mind, and Raj went for his pistol again. "Yo-yo-yo, Barz, I ain't on this sideways shit you obviously endorse," I yelled out, waving my hands in the air like *no go here*, not giving a fuck what none of his boy-loving homies thought. "I'm out of this studio, and if you want what you called me here for, you've got sixty seconds to meet me outside at my ride."

The music skipped as Raj and I walked out, but the freaky sex session that had set me off in the first place was still going strong. It was taking everything in me not to regurgitate. I ain't no homophobe, but I ain't tryin' to witness no nigga fuckin' and suckin' no nigga 'cause that's not how I roll. Raj had his heater in his hand and was talkin' cash shit about how a nigga better not even look at him wrong.

Without interference from the guard, we walked out of the studio and made it to the car without any interruption. Then Barz came strolling out the door. Pulling out a wad of cash, he held it up and asked if it was good for us to do business. I nodded, but his suspect ass couldn't get in my car.

Barz started explaining himself a few paces from the car. "First and foremost, that's them niggas and their swag, not mine. It kinda comes with the Hollywood territory, and part of the reason I be needing that girlie-girl you got."

"Nasty, man. Just fucking gross," Raj said. "I'ont give a fuck how much money them suit-wearing fools offer me to sign on the line. I ain't gonna be affiliated with no shit like that."

"Well, muthafucka, you do you, and I'ma do me, cashing them big checks all the way to the bank. I make more bread in a day of recording than you make hustling on the block all fuckin' month. Hell, year. Hell, fuck it—my bank account equals your life." Barz was going hard, hyped, and clearly off the girlie-girl he'd just proclaimed dabbing in so much.

Throwing my hand across Raj's chest so he'd stay in the car, I jumped in the middle of their argument to diffuse the beef before it went further. "Aye, Barz, lemme get a stack more on top of what you paid out the other night, and we're good. I'ma burn up outta here before you and my manz go at it, and the shit you got going on around here gets fucked up. You good, and we've been good, but this nigga here is my brother." I held the product out the window. He eagerly snatched it up, knowing there wasn't any negation on what I was saying and that my product would get him higher than a kite.

First paying the amount he'd initially paid last night, he then pulled out the additional stack needed for today's transaction. "Do you think we could step outside and speak about some business in private for a minute, Jayvon?" Barz pointed between me and him, excluding Raj. "No beef and I'm not on nothing tricky, but me and ya manz ain't like that." He didn't want my homeboy overhearing his conversation.

I got ready to tell Barz we were good and that our business was done because he and my ace bumped heads, but Raj stepped in and up. "Naw, we ain't like that, and I'm glad that fact is crystal clear," he addressed Barz and then me. "I'ma be cool and fall back so you can holla at that ol' Fruit-Loop nigga about getting that bread that's bigger than my life. Take ya time, bro."

I respected Raj for being bigger than the game.

"What's the word, Barz?" We were a few feet from the car, he with his back turned.

"I'm trying to spend a lot of money with you, Jayvon, not scrap with ya dude on no shit. I know these Hollywood cats be wild, but each of them spend racks daily on promethazine with codeine, pills, coke, whatever'll get 'em zoned the hell out and high." Barz started telling me how much money their current dealer was making but how weak and watered down his product was.

My mind was racing, thinking about all the benefits I'd reap from doing business with Barz. More money and connections to people with more money and status equated to a new level, something Morgan had been asking for. I'd be able to open her up another store, plus a li'l car wash that I could put a few li'l homies from around the hood to work in. Raj and Shylo could run it alongside me.

"*Think big. Do big. Live bigger.*" Morgan's voice sounded off in the back of my head. Unable to deny the truth of her words, I jumped at the opportunity.

"Well, as you've seen, getting you what you need ain't no thang. All you've gotta do is hit me up." I sealed the deal and shook on it, ready to run a check all the way up.

"A'ight, bet!" He handed me a handful of hundreds. "I was hoping you'd say that because I'm gonna need you to fall through with as many bottles of promethazine with codeine you can get your hands on, plus set up a candy shop for the gang so they can shop for themselves—all by tomorrow night, if possible. I've got a gig at the Underground we need to be lit at."

"Well, congratulations on ya gig—and for getting back in touch with me. What you need ain't a problem . . ." I started counting up the bread he'd passed over. "As long as you make sure your gang comes correct with that cash. This ain't nothing but a payment for a few bottles of syrup." I needed Barz and I to have a clear understanding.

"I wouldn't even had come to you on no sucker shit, bro. You're gonna be able to take your shorty shopping on Rodeo Drive after fuckin' with these cats. Their lifestyles might be funny, but their pockets ain't. They'll have your cash." He cosigned for them.

"Okay, well, hit me up when you and your team are ready to make moves." I was tired of hearing what the future could hold. If what he was selling could be bought, I'd see within forty-eight hours.

"Fa'sho. I got you." He caught my drift. "I'll be in touch. Until then, be easy."

"Yup, yup, you too." We dapped it up. Then Barz chucked up the deuces and walked back into the studio.

I climbed into the ride and reached for the blunt Raj was smoking. "Let me hit that, dog."

"Naw, homie." He jerked and snatched his hand back so I couldn't reach the blunt, damn near slamming himself into the door. "You're out here givin' handshakes and hugs after what we just saw in that studio—nawwww, you're good on this backwoods, bro." Raj was so serious. "At least until you wash your hands or put some antibacterial soap on 'em."

"Dogggg, you're a nut!" I started cracking up.

"Yeah, whatever. I've got paperwork on that—but what you won't say is that I'm into that fruity shit." He got comfortable in his seat again, never not once passing the wood.

Morgan

I loved quaint places; they comforted my spirit. I'd found this cozy coffee shop while scrolling the internet and had been eager to try it. I figured it would be the perfect place when I agreed to this study date. We were tucked off at a table in the back with textbooks open on the table, along with our highlighters and all the notes of Mrs. Harris's discourse during the last lecture. Even though I'd been nervous to be around Bryce, I was happy we were there. I was finally starting to focus on the material and getting a handle on the chapters. Bryce was in line getting us some more coffee and, this time, some bagels to go along with our session. The aroma of the freshly brewed coffee made me want it more. I was tired but still wanted to get some studying in.

My head was actually supposed to be in a book, but I was too busy watching Bryce's every move. For some reason, today, I was checking for him hard. He looked handsome in his Levi's, Polo-style shirt, and Cole Haan loafers. He looked clean, debonair, and like he was about to hop on the cover of a business-chic catalog or something. His style was much different than the thuggish swag I'd fallen in love with on Amp.

He ordered us some bagels and some more coffee, of course, then was on his phone. Even doing nothing at all, his stature held confidence. I couldn't help but wonder what was holding his attention on that phone because he kept being on it lately. Did he have a girl? Was he crushing on somebody? I shouldn't have cared . . . but I did. I was scared to admit I might've been crushing on his quirky ass, but I knew I was. I was getting butterflies every time we were together and even anticipating his messages. Bryce was so compassionate yet intriguing. There was something mysterious about him. I knew I was playing a dangerous game, but I felt I was playing it safe by creeping outside of our circle. There was no chance he and Amp could bump into each other.

Get it together, Morgan. Amp will kill you and him if he finds out. Through my thoughts, I kept a straight face. Now, he was walking toward me, smirking.

"Here you go, beautiful." He set down the tray. "I saw you over here checking for me. Is my outfit dripping?"

I burst out laughing. "Oh my God, you are so corny. Please don't say that again. I told you to be yourself, and it's cool. I went to school with preppy kids and overachievers my whole life."

"Really? What schools did you go to?"

"For elementary school, I went to St. Frances, about four hours away."

He was shocked I'd gone to the prestigious institution. "Wow, I've heard horror stories about that place. Like it's a baby boot camp."

"I can't speak for it now, but I'm sure it's the same. That place was a nightmare and strict as hell. It's probably more rigorous than a baby boot camp," I revealed.

We went from talking about schools to him questioning me about the boutique and what made me want to open it to him wanting to know if I drew up a business plan before making an initial move. Though I was careful not to mention Jayvon, our affiliations to the street, or the drug money I'd used to front all the merchandise, I did brag about my accomplishments and how I was growing the brand. I always went to Bryce for help, so it felt good to stand on a platform of achievement for a change. And it felt even better when he celebrated me.

"Wow! Opening up a business without having a college business course or at least a mentor to follow speaks volumes about how smart you are, Morgan. I am truly impressed by your determination." He was paying me compliments I didn't mind blushing for.

Jayvon might've helped get things running, but it had been my blood, sweat, tears, and hard work that made Sassy & Classy a fierce competitor. As much as I'd bumped heads with Jay about me going to school, it felt good getting my ego stroked by Bryce.

"Thanks so much for noticing my potential. I know it's hard to believe I'm a successful entrepreneur the way these grades are looking."

"Naw—not really. You're behind in class because you're a successful entrepreneur. There's a difference."

Once we started grinding and the personal questions stopped coming at me a mile a minute, I got more relaxed. We got more comfortable with each other.

The cafe started getting busier, and the space around us filled up. We were forced to pack up most of our books and study material, scooting closer together to keep our conversation going. It had been a while since I'd been able to talk openly about my dreams. I shared them with Bryce as well as hearing about his ambitions. With my guard down, I learned we had so much in common. The energy flowing between us was so intense, but in a good way. I knew we were slowly slipping out of the friend zone into a more intimate space, but I was okay with that.

"Wow, it seems like this place is a hit." A lady shook our table and almost spilled coffee on him, trying to slide by to the table beside us.

"Yeah, I guess so. Their coffee is delicious, though. Better than the big brand."

"I agree with you on that. I might have to come out of my way to grab us some cups before our next class."

"Although that would be nice, I need you in class on time. I won't be able to finish this semester without you."

"You absolutely will. We're almost at the goal line. I must admit I won't be sad when the semester ends, though I'll miss seeing your face," he shamelessly flirted.

"And I'll miss you making me smile," I confessed, not knowing if that was the right thing to do, but I couldn't help the words from slipping out of my lips.

"We could have more time than that if you quit stalling and give a brother some play." He bluntly stated what he wanted. "You know I'm feeling you, Morgan."

It was time to quit going around in circles and address Bryce about him trying to cuff me. But I was cut short by a dark cloud that seemed to loom over me suddenly. I looked up . . . and my jaw dropped to the floor as my mother's eyes locked with mine. We hadn't seen each other in years, and I could tell time hadn't been on her side. Her mocha skin had wrinkled, her usually toned body was about twenty pounds heavier, and her hair which usually stayed beautifully done, had broken off badly. The stiff curls didn't have any bounce or shimmer. She looked rough and worn out.

"Stay put," she mouthed to my father, throwing her arm across his chest, and I saw him budge, which made me look at him in pity.

I could see worry and stress all over his face. He was still weak for her after all this time. I always favored my father because he was the nicer of the two. He catered to me the way a father should to his baby daughter but failed to stand up for me when it came to his wife. He let her run shit, right or wrong, then do something nice for me behind her back to help me feel better. I appreciated the gestures because it was better than living in complete hell, but I would've appreciated it more had he stood up for me and shut down her parenting methods.

I loved my dad, but he just didn't have any bark. That might've been why I gravitated toward Jayvon as well. He commanded attention. Demanded his respect. I already knew I couldn't pull no slick shit with our kid if we ever did have a baby. Raw, rough, and rugged—I knew he would be a good father because he too wanted the exact opposite of what he had growing up.

Time stood still, giving one of us time to say something—but only silence consumed us. Just like I only had one mom and one dad, they only had one child and daughter—me.

"Earth to Morgan, are you okay?"

I heard Bryce trying to get my attention and even saw him waving his hand in front of my face, but my expression was stuck like stone and focused head-on. Not being able to get me to answer, Bryce finally followed my gaze and gasped. He must've noticed the resemblance of the woman off rip. I was a miniature version of my momma.

"Are those your parents, Morgan? Do you need me to give you a second?" Bryce questioned, grabbing my head and rubbing it.

A few more uncomfortable seconds passed, and still, no words were exchanged. All eyes were on me, even Bryce's. Everyone wanted a reaction, but all I could give them was my ass to kiss as I ran out the door.

"Okay, Morgan, breathe. You've gotta breathe." I sat behind the steering wheel, trying to calm my anxiety so I could try starting the car to get the fuck out of Dodge.

I couldn't handle a face-to-face meeting with my parents. I wasn't ready for whatever their opinion of me was, especially if it was the same shitty one they'd given to me when I chose my heart's decision over the one they'd planned out for me. I'd lived the boring, suburban life. I was forced into ballet, piano lessons, etiquette classes, and even boarding school for half my elementary years. I was being groomed to be seen and not heard, elegant and intelligent, dainty and proper. But all that went out the window once I started blooming into a teenager. I started forming my own opinions and pushing back on all that old-school "way of a woman" garbage they were forcing down my throat and pushing to have a voice. I began raising hell at the private institutions. That's how I ended up at a public school in the city. I was feenin' for fresh-air freedom. Jayvon was all the thrills I'd been missing my whole life.

I knew I'd hurt them by going against the grain, but it hurt me ten times more being disowned all these years. In the hood, I'd seen many broken families that suffered worse traumatic events rip them apart and come back together. Even drug-addicted mothers and fathers tried their best to keep their skeletons tucked in the closet for their kids' emotional well-being. But my parents had money, stocks even, and they stooped lower than low and threw rocks at me. I wholeheartedly understood they might've been disappointed by my decision, but nothing in this world would make me understand or digest all the rejection.

Chapter 20

Morgan

The next day, class went well and ended on a great note. And it probably helped that Bryce was absent so I didn't have to answer anything about the situation at the coffee shop. I was still full of anxiety and on edge from yesterday. Even Amp picked up on that energy.

I needed a positive demeanor and personality for my day at the boutique, which had been going well so far. Sassy & Classy was booming with business. It was jam-packed with people taking advantage of the sale I'd been promoting all month. I couldn't have been happier. All the studying and talking to my professor about market-ing and increasing my sales was finally paying off. This was definitely the direction I wanted to go in.

The faces of my customers turned to dollar signs as I surveyed everyone shopping. Every square foot of the shop Jayvon gifted me was filled to capacity. I'd certainly be up all night ordering new merchandise at the rate clothes were flying off the racks. It was a good thing I'd thought ahead and ordered a few items ahead of time. With the number of likes, retweets, and shares I was getting on social media, I couldn't help but be optimistic.

Nakeya's section of the boutique had more of a crowd than the shopping area did. Chicks were trying to get fitted for dresses, strip costumes, and their vision of a generic creation of a name-brand created.

Because Keya liked to make sure she got all the measurements and particulars absolutely correct, she didn't have an assistant and was a one-woman army. My girl was busting out in a sweat trying to sew costumes and take orders at the same time. I couldn't throw shade, though. As heavy as her workload was, she never missed a deadline.

I didn't want to take money out of her pocket, especially because she'd had my back regarding my personal life with Jayvon, but I was thinking about adding another seamstress to our team. With my business doing numbers, I knew someone would soon copy my idea. That meant I needed to capitalize on the monopoly I had going. My brand was everything. I had a list of ways to make sure my business and I became established, and I was dead set on implementing them one by one.

Adding another seamstress meant my boutique could handle more business. The more customers I pleased, the greater my potential for a referral and their repeat business. The moves I was making weren't for a short-term investment but for stability in my future. Jayvon thought he'd have to stay married to the street. I was dead set on showing him so much more.

"Would you like to purchase some lipstick or accessories to match your outfit? I'll give you a special deal—buy one, get one 50 percent off."

She passed, but that was okay. I made the sale on her clothes anyway. When the line slowed down at the register, I moved from behind the counter and started pushing for more sales on the floor. The same way I'd been hungry for niggs to buy my package in the hood, I was thirsty to be a legal entrepreneur. If this shit popped and paid me the same amount I collected in the streets, I could retire sooner than later. I was tired of looking over my shoulder.

"Drinks on you tonight . . . because I know you're taking us out after slaving us all day." Jos walked up, pinching me.

"Girl, bye! You see how empty my racks and shelves are? I'll be doing stock all night. The most I can do is buy a bottle and turn up the music in here for y'all." Continuing to pick up clothes that had fallen, I was too busy grinding in work mode to be thinking about partying.

"I swear you ain't no fun no more," Jos complained. "If you ain't caking with Jayvon, yo' ass is doing homework or running this place. It ain't gonna kill you to live a little. Damn."

"Yo' ass wouldn't be able to eat and have fun if I didn't grind," I responded. "So get back to work and earn the paycheck I'll be signing at the end of the week," I trumped her.

Jos huffed but didn't put up a fuss. "I'ma get my ass back to work, Miss Morgan Massa, but I'ma need my liquor as soon as I punch out."

Business continued to bang until I locked the door while the last handful of shoppers were getting rung up. Nakeya was finally up from behind her sewing station for the first time today and was sweeping up. We were all tired but also ready to celebrate today's success. I'd promised to pay them bonuses today if business banged, and from the numbers, we fa'sho did that. I was already at the computer pulling up websites to restock.

"Girl, I've got more orders than I know what to do with," Nakeya excitedly spoke, finally acting all the way back to herself.

We hadn't really had a moment to ourselves since the boutique had been popping as I walked in from school.

"Yeah, I don't see how you keep coming up with one-of-a-kind designs with all the outfits you sew. I admire your skill." I paid her a genuine compliment.

"Thanks, baby doll. I thank my granny every single day for teaching me how to sew. She used to have me threading all her needles before she could afford a sewing machine. I was the only little girl in my neighborhood with custom-made Barbie doll clothes." Nakeya was lost in a happy memory, and you could tell from how bright her eyes were.

This probably wasn't the best time to bring up my thoughts about hiring another seamstress, but I had to keep it real. Besides, this wasn't a personal move to slight her. It was all about business.

"Sis, I've been thinking about bringing in another girl to help with all the clientele we've been getting for custom orders." I was blunt and direct.

"Um, what? Why would you do that? Me and you had a deal, and I thought shit was going sweet. I thought you recognized you lost ya mind and found it from the other night. What the fuck is this sneak attack tip you on now?"

I hadn't expected Nakeya to jump at the idea of welcoming another girl, but I didn't expect her to jump crazy, either. "Okay, before I respond, let me tell you I wasn't trying to slight you or play the disloyal card. I apologized, meant it, and this has nothing to do with your brand release party. I ain't petty. As far as I'm concerned, we're good, and I hope we stay that way. You're one of my best friends. Now, to the part that pisses you off, I considered hiring another girl to get more customers. From a business standpoint, the more orders we can take—the more money we can make. And I know your hungry ass wanna eat."

I thought that would ease the tension with Nakeya, but it didn't. When her neck snapped back, rolled, and she rolled her eyes damn near up into her head, I knew me and my girl were about to beef. And from my angle, there wasn't a reason for that.

"*I'm* the one who helped you bring bitches through the door." Nakeya started tapping her foot like she was revving up to go hard on me. "Now that you've counted up the stripper money I've been counting for years, you wanna cut a bitch down for a few dollars? Them stripper chicks that put money in your pocket are my friends, and if I ain't fuckin' with you, they won't." She was going off.

"Wow, Keya. For real?" I was shocked, flabbergasted, and thrown back.

"Hell yeah, for real. Your reasoning seems fake, rushed, and made up. I hope this ain't no shade from me not answering your calls over the weekend, 'cause this shit don't make no sense. I don't see you dragging another assistant in here for Jos's drop-the-ball ass. It's always a gang of girls in here waiting to be helped. Plus, it ain't never a day I'm not here with the ma'fucking birds when yo' ass up under Jayvon's ass like a turd."

"Don't pull me in y'all shit," Jos loudly interjected, walking in with a bag from the store and a bouquet of yellow flowers.

I looked at her weirdly, like, "Why do you have a bouquet?" I couldn't question it because Nakeya needed a reply.

"Look, Nakeya, I ain't trying to argue with you, nor am I trying to get anything jumping between all of us. It was just an idea. Now that you know my thoughts, make a move and get yourself an assistant or an apprentice. That way, you can continue to keep all the money to yourself, have control over the assistant, and fill more orders. I'm about to make some moves with marketing that'll bring more bitches on top of the bitches you've brought through the door, so we'll need the help." I put it like she put it to me—using the word "bitches."

The tension in her shoulders dropped. I'd said the words that relaxed her. She was uptight, overly thinking I wanted to take control.

"Okay, cool. That sounds more like it. I'll start the interview process to find the perfect person."

"Fine. Looks like we can continue counting stripper money together." I was being sarcastic.

She rolled her eyes, then picked up her glass of liquor, making a toast to me. "Cheers!"

"Uh-uh. I don't care that y'all two wannabe divas ain't at each other necks no more, but I'm still pissed at you, Nakeya. Why'd you call me out like that?" Jos looked salty. "Oh yeah, and by the way, those flowers are for you, Morgan. Now, back to you, Nakeya—answer me."

Falling back, I sipped my wine and got back to ordering merchandise. They could keep that argument to themselves. I didn't even bother looking at the flowers because I knew they were from Jayvon trying to apologize for all the bullshit I'd gone through the other day. Though I told him I accepted his apology, he'd been giving me gifts ever since.

Once I was done ordering everything I could find, I thanked everyone who supported me via social media. Then I got out my to-do list to update it. That was another good habit I'd learned from my professor. The more things I accomplished and could cross off as completed, the more I added. Losing wasn't an option, but coming up was.

Tallying up today's earnings, I'd divvied up stacks for Jos, Nakeya, and even myself. Since there was more than enough left over, I decided to do some upgrading to my shop. I'd been researching online different boutiques in other cities and designs I could decorate mine in and was ready to give Sassy & Classy a face-lift. Before I ended up spending the money or ordering more stuff, I started the process.

I ordered a chic couch, a few fancy decorative pillows that I could make some DIY posters I'd YouTube to match, and a plush-looking area rug off Amazon that I got for the low-low. The lounge area I was decorating in my mind would be sweet. At least, I hoped it would be.

"Here, Morgan, let me fill your glass up to the top," Jos said, leaning over my shoulder. "What are you ordering furniture for? Here?"

"Yup, I'm even going to paint. I'm finally going to turn that space near the dressing room into a chic lounge area." I started to run off all my ideas.

"Oh, okay, that sounds cute. If you really wanna get it popping in here, though, you should get a pole on a small stage in the center of that lounge area. That way, the girls can try on their outfits and dance in the mirror at the same time." She did a few sexy dance moves to imitate how they'd be. Nakeya and I giggled at her. "What? Y'all can quit laughing at my idea. Think about it, Morgan. We already give 'em glasses of wine to loosen them up to spend more money. If they had access to a pole too, they'd have fun up in here. You know we'd always have a friendly competition going down in here on that pole with all the stripper chicks who buy our clothes. That means people will linger longer to see what's popping. The longer they linger, the more probability it'll be that they'll buy something." Jos kicked her knowledge, sounding like me. Her idea actually resonated with me.

"Wow, you're actually on to something. Not only could I add a stage and pole, but I could also hold classes here at least one night a week too. The girls could pay the dancer instructing them, but nothing to us. We'll make our money on the flip with costumes and merchandise."

"Aw, shit naw! You're gonna have to hire me an assistant in a minute," Jos joked, swinging her neck in Nakeya's direction.

"Ha-ha," Keya replied, ready to go word for word with Jos if needed.

"Okay, you two. We're all about to get money, and we're not the type of friends who compete for money. Cool?"

"Cool." Keya was the first to respond. "I'll toast to that."

"Me too. Two whole shots." Jos tightened our friendship circle.

Since all the work I'd planned was done, I turned the overhead speakers on with a mix CD I'd gotten from the gas station. It was a compilation of today's latest R&B songs. Jos made sure our glasses were filled to the brim. Then we all kicked back, singing along, showing each other dance moves in the mirror, and gossiping. With my hectic life, I needed more chill time like this with my girls.

"Heyyy, bro," Nakeya slurred as soon as she saw Amp walk in. She was hella lit.

"Damn, I see y'all been turning up." He picked up one of the bottles of wine we'd been sipping from, then looked at me. "Are you fucked up too?"

"Naw, I'm good, baby." I got up, putting my arms around him. He looked good as hell dressed in an all-white Gucci 'fit, with his ice jumping off the crispness, blinding me. "Where are you about to go through?" I pulled back.

"We are about to go to a gig Barz put me down with. It's out in the burbs. One of his industry friends is having it, so you've gotta go get dolled up."

"Wow, you could've given me some notice." I started panicking, not knowing what I was about to wear or how I was about to get myself together so quickly. Today had been my chill day, so I was in sweats, no makeup, with my hair pulled into a pony.

"You work in a beauty bar. Pull one of those dresses off the mannequin, then paint your face or whatever you girls say. The shit shouldn't be that hard," he shrugged.

"Nakeya, help ya girl with glam while I roll up. You got one hour, Mooka." Amp walked off to the back where my office was like he hadn't dropped a feat on me.

"Well, girl, you heard what your husband said. Get a dress off the mannequin, and let's transform you into a bad bitch. This is exactly what Sassy & Classy is for." She pushed me toward the showroom floor.

An hour later, Nakeya wasn't only a stylist, but she had my weave pressed bone straight and flowing down my back like a goddess. Neither of us wanted to play on my face with makeup, so we kept it simple with a basic beat of eyeshadow, some lashes, and, of course, a pretty pink-tinted gloss. It was an angelic, soft look. And so was my outfit. I matched Amp's fly in a spaghetti-strapped white dress that stopped an inch above my knees and had feathers around the bottom. It was simple yet sexy, clinging on to every curve I'd been blessed and fucked into having. Amp's eyes lit up when he saw me strut into my office in the six-inch silver-strapped stilettos. He loved me in heels, always saying it made my ass sit up fatter.

"I see you're ready to go, Mrs. Banks." He got up, eying me with lust. I knew he wanted to fuck. But for as quickly as I had to get glammed up, he'd have to wait.

"Yes, I am, Mr. Banks. And I love the way that sounds— Mrs. Banks." I locked hands with him, and then we leaned in for a kiss.

"And I love the way it sounds rolling off my lips. Let's bounce, baby."

Jayvon

It was late as hell, and I wasn't trying to be out in the burbs, but Barz had a homeboy trying to get some gallons of syrup, and I wasn't about to miss out on the money.

Barz wasn't lying when he said I could be a celebrity supplier. His connects were already about to put hella bands in my pocket. As we pulled up to the extravagant mini-mansion, I slid my pistol from my waistband to underneath the seat. Me and my girl were looking good, smelling good, and to be rubbing shoulders with the rich and famous, there wasn't a need for me to be strapped.

"I see you over there thinking, all mesmerized by these cribs." I called shorty out of her thoughts.

"Yeah, you know I love these houses, Amp. I'd go all HGTV crazy, decorating all day like a housewife if I had one of these homes."

"Yo' ass ain't about to cook no food, though." That's one thing my baby wasn't a master at . . . getting down in the kitchen. I was the one who could cook. "You know what? I'll be honest with you. It wouldn't be so bad whipping up some work in one of these Master Chef-ass kitchens with a chef hat on."

"Boy, bye. You are crazy." She burst out laughing. "Be for real."

"I am being for real. It would be dope to have BBQs and invite the hood out to this bitch to blow it out. Then I know you'd wanna have your li'l homegirls over to swim."

"Yup, you're damn right. I would. But you're playing, and I'm really serious. We can't keep doing all this hustling just to stay stagnant. I want up out of the hood. I want this right here. I saw a for sale sign up the street."

"Whoa, on ease, baby girl. We're not even 'bout to be neighbors with the connect. But I hear you, and I'm not playing. You know I'm not the best with my words, but I just wanted you to know I appreciate you for holding me down and just being solid with a nigga all the way around. I know it ain't easy thuggin' it out with me sometimes."

"You're welcome, and you know I'm always going to have your back—but I really want you to consider all the preaching I've been doing about switching up how we hustle and operate. At the end of the day, all I want is longevity with you and for us to start moving differently. This street shit been getting reallll grimy, and I don't want to lose you to the game or get caught up. We can hustle on the books and still bank hella bread, bae."

"Just give yo' man some time to handle some live pieces out here." I knew that was not what she wanted to hear, but that's all I could give now. Tonight, though, I was about to try to be the polished nigga she wanted me to be.

"Mrs. Banks." I extended my arm so she could slide hers into mine. Then it seemed like she was floating on air to the mansion.

I couldn't even front. As soon as we walked through the doors, I was thrown back. This extravagant ritzy shit was kinda fly as fuck. Huge artwork hung on the walls that I knew cost a grip, chandeliers dripped in crystal hung from the ceiling, and there were gray and white marble floors throughout.

"Madam." One of the workers appeared, and then a woman handed Morgan a Champagne flute filled to the brim. Afterward, they greeted me with a tray holding two drinks, light and dark, and, of course, I went for the Crown Royal. Waitresses moved throughout the party with Champagne bottles, liquor trays, and even coke lines for those who wanted to dabble. That's one thing about rich muthafuckas. They could party with drugs right out in the open, and nobody blinked an eye. If this was a hood party, the only thing we'd be blowing on was tree, and doing that looking over our shoulders just in case a ho-ass cop wanted to be on some petty shit.

"What have you brought me to, Amp?" Morgan whispered in my ear while her eyes continued dancing around the room.

"To dine on fine cuisine and bump elbows with the wealthy, darling." I put on my classy man voice, then led her into the main room, where everyone was gathered. I was sure the host of the night was amongst his guests. And he was. He had his head dipped off in one of the trays, sniffing up a whole line of cocaine like it was mere water to quench his thirst.

"He must be who we're here to see." Morgan picked up on the mark just as quickly.

"Yup. One of the moving pieces I was referring to. With clients like him, we can really afford all this shit he affording. This is where the money is at, baby."

She nodded in agreement.

Chapter 21

Morgan

The smell of salmon and rice hit my nostrils when I woke up. It was Jayvon in the kitchen throwing down. He hadn't cooked us a meal in forever. Though I wanted to think it was for a special occasion, I knew Jayvon was trying to keep me happy. Either that, or he was trying to cover up something. I knew him too well.

Barely sitting up straight, my energy was in the tank from staying up all night, trapping with Jayvon. Once we returned from clinking wineglasses and selling nose candy, we'd stopped by the trap house to restock. Looking at the clock, I saw it was only 11:00 a.m., which meant we'd only been asleep for about four hours. The sun was shining by the time our heads hit the pillow. I probably wouldn't be up now if it weren't for Jayvon not being in bed. The boutique didn't open for a few more hours, and I didn't have a class for the day.

Sliding on my robe, I waltzed into the kitchen, enjoying the aroma of deliciousness every step of the way. The way my stomach was grumbling, I was about to smash every morsel he put on my plate. Jayvon had always been known to make moves in the kitchen. If Valerie didn't teach him nothing else, she fa'sho taught him that.

Not saying a word, I stood still and watched Jayvon from behind. He was standing over the stove scrambling eggs, but it looked like he was whippin' that work. His thuggish ass was turning me the hell on, and he didn't even know it. Feeling like a nigga must feel when watching a chick cook in high heels and boy shorts, I got horny and wanted to pounce on his ass for some sex. All the hours of him bench pressing, doing crunches, and push-ups had paid off big time. His muscular, tattooed arms were bulging from out of his wife beater.

Quietly tiptoeing up on him, I ran my hand across his back, finally making my presence known. "Good morning, bae."

"'Sup, boo?" He turned and kissed me on the mouth, morning breath and all. We'd done a lot nastier things to each other sexually, so it wasn't nothing. "G'on and fire up that blunt on the table. Breakfast is about to be ready."

"A girl can get used to this. You're pulling out all the surprises this morning, huh? What do I owe the pleasure of this 'B and B'?" I'd nicknamed the session denoting blunt and breakfast.

"Because you deserve it, and I'm trying to start our day without fighting since we're actually waking up together."

I smacked my lips, not trying to get pacified with a hot plate of food. "Yeah, I feel you. I wanna be happy all day, though, not just for the few minutes we eat breakfast."

Taking his attention off the skillets on the stove, he turned around and responded. "I ain't in the mood for your fast-talking lips this morning, especially when I'm trying to make amends with you. Please do me a favor and be cool. It's starting to feel like a nigga can't win for losing with ya ass."

"Fine." I dropped the subject. Flicking the flame to the lighter, I lit up the cigarillo and took my first big puff of the day. The dense smoke clouded my chest, quickly erasing whatever gall was building up to argue with Jayvon. We ate and smoked in silence until his phone rang.

"Yo, talk to me," Jayvon answered, still smacking.

After listening for a few seconds, I was all too eager to leave Jayvon to his phone call. I wanted to see if Bryce had messaged me back from last night. After the flower incident, I'd powered it off and tossed it into my purse.

Turning on the shower, I sat on the toilet and let out a few streams of urine while my phone powered up. My coochie felt a little sore from all the sex we'd been having, so I turned on the bath instead and dropped a capful of alcohol into the water along with some vinegar. Along with the piping hot water, my vagina would be soothed and tightened back up in no time.

By the time my phone finished loading all the notifications from my personal and business social network pages, I was soaking in the tub. Ignoring every other alert, I opened my messaging application and saw Bryce's reply bolded. He'd sent a total of four messages. I read them from the most recent to the latest.

Bryce: I guess I'll give you your space. See you in class.

Bryce: Um . . . I ain't trying to pester you . . . but can you at least reply yes or no . . . I really don't want us to be on bad terms.

Bryce: Morgan? Do you accept my apology? Did I overstep my boundaries again?

Bryce: The flowers were because I overstepped my boundaries with what I said. I didn't mean to make you mad. I apologize.

Instead of telling him I thought the gesture was nice and that I accepted his apology, I let the messages continue lingering and called Jos to find out what the card within the flowers said. What I should've done, though, was dead the whole interaction between Bryce and me and maybe even drop the class until next semester. It was not like I was excelling anyway. The fact that I was grinning like a kid while reading his messages and waiting anxiously for Jos to answer the phone meant I was straddling the fence. I was, in fact, crushing back on the nerd that was crushing on me. Damn.

Jos answered on the first ring, amped like it was the middle of the day. "Uh-huh, I've been waiting on you to call. You've got some nigga feenin' for you for real. Who in the hell is Bryce? Huh? Gimmie the tea, bitch, 'cause you been obviously holding out."

Hearing her saying he was feenin' for me made me blush. "I'll fill you in later, Jos. I promise. Tell me what the card said, though."

She smacked her lips. "Fine. I'll read it to you, but whoever this Rico Suave nigga is, don't go fuck with him and mess up what I just got going with Raj. If you and Jayvon fall out, I'ma have a hard time keeping Raj on my team. You know how the crew rolls."

"Oh, so that means you must've gotten you some last night?" I addressed what she said about her and Raj, not her advice to me.

"Girl, yes. And that man got a muthafuckin' monster," she excitedly screamed in my ear, amped up off the dick. "I damn near passed out, choked, and lost my life trying to handle him, but I did, and I will again. I think I'm in love."

I burst out laughing. "Make sure I'm the matron of honor at the wedding."

"Uh-uh, I don't know about that. After Jayvon breaks your legs for cheating on him, you won't be getting wheeled down no wedding line of mine," she vainly spat.

"Bitch, shut up."

"Naw, shut ya'self up. Matter of fact, I won't be a coconspirator to fuckin' up a relationship I want. You wanna know what ol' boy put on the card, you call him yourself. Bye." She hung up the phone in my face. I was shocked and kinda pissed but had to laugh it off. I couldn't and wasn't about to hate on my girl.

Leaning back on the towel, I closed my eyes and thought about Bryce. I really, really, really wished I knew what the card said. I'd snapped at him in school, but I think that was because I hadn't admitted being attracted to him. Ever since I'd been opening up to him, I'd been closing down on Jayvon. And I couldn't help it. Bryce had been tending to a side of me that Jayvon had been refusing to accept.

Wishing I hadn't gone off on him . . . wishing I'd chosen a different set of words and presentation of them, I was one finger motion away from calling him. My finger was on "send" when Jayvon barged through the bathroom door. I'd forgotten to lock it, something I'd remember to do from now on. Fumbling with my phone, I almost dropped it in the tub of water. "Dang, bae, you could've given me a warning you were coming in. I almost dropped my phone," I whined.

"I didn't think I needed to announce myself in my muthafuckin' house." He eyed me suspiciously, making me realize I was giving him a reason to.

"You don't. You just scared me because I thought you were still eating breakfast with ya big greedy ass. That's all," I tried reasoning. "But anyway, since you didn't make me drop my phone, are you ready? I didn't get a chance to toss some overnight clothes into a bag, but that won't take but a second."

"Something came up, so it's gonna be a few hours."

I rolled my eyes with attitude, then climbed out of the tub. "Here we go. You're good for a few days, only to revert right back to the dumb shit. I knew it."

"It ain't like that, so don't start."

"Yeah, whatever. Say that shit to ya'self in the car to wherever it is you're going."

Jayvon didn't respond. He was too busy walking out the door.

"Oh, well. On to the next." I said the last part under my breath, watching him out the window.

As soon as he pulled out of the driveway, I shouldn't have run back into the bathroom for my phone to call Bryce, but I did. I was out of breath waiting on him to pick up, but he didn't. His voicemail kept popping on. After the first two times, I took a break from calling and reviewed my text messages to reread what he'd sent. I then checked my voicemails to hear his messages again. I was looking for a reason why he'd be ignoring me, but smiling through each of his messages made me do the exact opposite, from deleting his number to calling him back three more times. All out of character, I was anxious to talk to this man who wasn't my man. I would've kept calling had he not powered off his phone. At this point, you couldn't tell me he wasn't ignoring me. I kinda felt some sort of way.

Opening my textbooks to study, I read through the entire assigned chapter without retaining a word or theory. Bryce was on my mind. Jayvon was on my mind. Why I was allowing Bryce to be on my mind was on my mind. I was going stir-crazy. Grabbing my keys and purse, I darted out the door for some fresh air.

Chapter 22

Amp

I pulled up to Shylo's crib. He was on the porch smoking a leaf of Kush and drinking a Gatorade.

"What up, fam? You good from the club? I ain't heard from you." I walked up, and he passed me the leaf. The buds were hitting harder than a muthafucka as they invaded my lungs.

"Hell naw, but I will be. Them hoes were coming for my pockets hard last night. When I woke up, I counted up my knot and was short about three bands." He rubbed the sweat off his head like it was getting to him that he'd blown so much cash—and I didn't blame him.

"Damn, bro. I knew you got off on these broads but not like that off last night, but I didn't know it was like that." I'd spent only half of what he'd counted up, and I'd purchased bottles too. "That's a lot of chicken to spend on some hoes that ain't slob knobbin' and taking it to the guts."

"Who the fuck you telling?" He got up and entered the house, and I followed him.

"What up wit' you, fam? I'm shocked yo' ass is alive after last night. Ol' girl you left with was bad as hell and murdering you for that money."

"That broad wasn't nothing but a performer. Her pussy was whack as hell." He sat down at the table with us and started doing his thang. "The only reason I didn't put her out of my spot is 'cause it didn't stink. She's gonna be mad as hell when I see her and don't speak, but I'on even give a fuck. She shouldn't be out here tricking niggas and shit. I could've hooked up with one of my old shorties and been super straight."

I was laughing hard as hell at Raj because he was dead serious. "You a nut, bro. You probably could've went home with Morgan's homegirl Keya 'cause she was feeling you from what I've heard."

"Yo, straight up? Shiiiit, text my sis and tell her to throw them digits at her bro."

Shylo bent down and snorted up a line of pill powder he'd just finished grinding down. "Fuck, yeah, I can flip this shit for higher. It's most definitely stronger. Bump half a line off all them baggies. They ain't even gonna be able to tell because this shit hits harder." He sounded like a tester instead of the seller he was supposed to be.

He then tilted up a Gatorade and guzzled almost the entire bottle down. I knew at that point he wasn't low-key hungover from Nita's drinks last night but fighting dehydration from rolling all night. That's why his ass was acting wild and had tricked off all his cash. Pure MDMA is notorious for sucking a pill popper's internal water supply dry, and our product was hitting on damn near 100 percent. Fam wasn't outside catching a breeze when I pulled up but waiting like a fiend for some more product.

"You a nut, cuzzo. Damn. You kinda got me spent 'cause I didn't know you was popping these boys." I thought back to when Morgan suggested Shylo was acting weird and giving her odd vibes last night, like he was off on some shit stronger than weed and liq, but I'd dismissed it. I didn't want to hear that my blood family was getting bent—and it was blowing my mind that I'd witnessed him snort it up like it was nothing.

"You ain't gotta worry. I'm solid. I only fucks with this shit here and there."

"That's one time too many, don't you think?" I was heated at how nonchalant he was being and how dumb he was acting. "We sell that shit because it's addictive, and you think it's a good idea to start fucking with it? Where's yo' head at? I can't be moving with you if you moving with the other side." Initially, I was chill with the conversation until Shylo started moving funny and tensing up. I loved him like my brother, but I wouldn't hesitate to beat his ass. I was praying I didn't have to send my auntie shopping for a black dress.

"Yo! Ay-yooo!" Raj came into the house to see me and Shylo mean mugging each other, waiting for the first move. "I left y'all alone for five seconds. What happened?"

"Oh, it's smooth, fam." I was talking to Raj but staring at Shylo. "I was just in here letting this nigga know you were going to make the Penn run instead of him this go-round."

"You're a ho-ass nigga for this move." Shylo's nose flared as he balled his fists up like he was ready to swing over Raj.

"This shit be helping me stay up for the drive and to get them off once I'm there. I can't be falling asleep at the wheel or taking no naps all leisurely and shit like I'm not a drug dealer." He was running down a bunch of reasons why he was popping pills, but they only translated to "Keep a watch on me."

"Oh . . . okay then. I got you." I decided to temporarily fall off the subject until I had a chance to holla at Raj about taking over the runs on his own. Fam was still fam, but I wasn't about to be supplying Shylo's habit or taking a risk with my money and the connections I'd built out of town on a pillhead—period! It was low-key fuckin' me up in the head that he thought I was buying his bullshitting-ass story.

Shylo didn't work for Rich when we were li'l niggas, so he didn't see firsthand how all the crackheads used to be rockin' around Rich's crib when they were off his Rich Boys. I'd heard some wild-ass stories from people who used to want credit until their checks rolled in and seen some even wilder shit take place when people wanted to work off their debts. And just like my b-ball coach was one of them, a nursery school teacher was too. A monkey will get on anyone's back. Trust and believe that with your heart. I had to holla at Valerie on how to handle this nigga.

Raj

I wasn't about to get in the middle of Shylo and Amp's beef. Them niggas were blood, and I wasn't shit but an outsider invited into the fold at the end of the day. I mean—I had mad love for them, especially since they'd always rocked one hundred with me, but I learned a long time ago that love came with conditions when my mother dropped me off and gave up her rights to me. That happened to me over ten years ago, and I still wasn't over it.

I knew Shylo was dipping off in the packages and popping pills. Not only did I know a head when I saw one, but I also still had side effects from all the antipsychotic drugs my moms medicated me with to get me to act right. I knew the signs because I used to go through the motions too. I could drink two gallons of water straight out of the jug when I was a kid—and still be feenin' for something to drink. Again, that wasn't my monkey to fight. The only thing I was out here trying to do was get money.

"'Sup? Let me get this on pump four." I slid a fifty spot through the slot. "I'll be back for my change 'cause that li'l shit shouldn't even take all of that."

I walked out of the gas station and to the Chevy Cruz I was about to be cramped as hell in for hours. We never used trucks when we did runs because the boys would be quick to assume we were packing that bitch. While the gas pumped, I smoothed out the University of Michigan bumper sticker across the bumper and replaced the rental car's license plate holder with the blue and gold plate holder that repped U of M.

"Yo, you 'bout to hit the road, Raj?" Shylo asked, calling.

"Yeah, I'm filling up the shooter right now."

"You know I'll take that ride for you. Fuck what Amp talking 'bout. He ain't our boss." Shylo was getting loud and way too emotional to be talking about going on the road with some product.

"Naw, man, I'm straight. I need to hit the road and clear my head about some shit anyway."

"Yeah, a'ight, but it's still fuck Amp. I'm getting tired of him thinking he run shit. We all been putting in work. We all equal. Partners."

"I hear you, Shylo, but you know I ain't getting in that shit. That's family business, blood business, not my business." I kept it a buck with my homeboy. Always have and always will.

"I can respect that, but just know you gonna have to pick a side sooner than later. I'ma get at you. Be safe out there." He hung up, and I was quick to put the nigga on my block list. He was giving off weird energy that I didn't need for this type of road trip. I needed my focus up on a thousand.

I cranked the engine and jumped on the highway. Thanks to our inside connect, the car was already packed with the work when I pulled it off the rental lot.

"Yo, Amp, man, I gotta holla at you about some shit, and I really don't want this coming back at me because it's about your fam." I had to tell him what was up. I had a weird feeling about how Shylo was acting.

"You already know you're fam, so I ain't looking at shit different. What's good?"

"Shylo just hit me up some 'fuck Amp, let me still hit the lick type shit.' He starting to get too wild, my dude."

"Say less. We there. He moving funny, and that nose-dipping can't be trusted. We'll talk when you get back. I got shit under control till you get back. Then we can link up to see how to handle things and move forward."

"Bet." I was satisfied, ready to concentrate on the road and work on my flows. I wasn't a rapper, nor was I trying to be. It was just my way of tuning out all this street static I was involved in.

Jayvon

"Yo, Ma, where you at?" I used my key and walked into my mom's crib.

"In my room getting dressed," she called out. "Come back here so we can talk. I need to run something past you."

"A'ight, let me piss real quick." I took care of myself in the bathroom, washed my hands, then went to check out what was in the kitchen to eat. My stomach was grumbling like a big dog.

Valerie had never been a cooker, but she always had leftover carryout food and loaded up to-go containers from the casino. When I was a kid, she'd load up the cabinets with microwavable ravioli, my favorite cereals, macaroni, grits, and Ramen noodles. And the fridge had milk, lunch meat, hot dogs, bread, cheese, and microwavable bacon. Every now and then, she'd fry some chicken, bake some hot wings, or broil steaks. But I never complained about not having traditional meals. I knew women who sold their WIC benefits, and that wasn't shit but milk, eggs, dry beans, and a few dollars of fruits and vegetables. Big V was many things, but she ain't never let my black ass go hungry for a hit.

I found some chicken alfredo from Olive Garden, popped it into the microwave, then went into her room, chowing down.

"What up with you, Ma?" I plopped down on the bed and made myself comfortable.

"What up with me, my ass!" She turned from the mirror and looked at me like I wasn't welcome. "Get your dirty ass up off my bed, boy. And why are you eating my food?"

"I was hungry, Ma. Dang!" I kept stuffing my face.

"Then take your hungry ass home to your uppity girl-friend. I don't care that she serves you pretty plates with petty portions, and yo' ass is starving."

"C'mon, Ma. Chill. It's really getting old that you keep coming for my girl." I was tired of the drama between her and Morgan. She'd never liked my girl, and it wasn't based on nothing but the fact that she was bougie and came from money.

She shrugged her shoulders nonchalantly. "It's getting old to you and her, but I'm good with it."

I kept eating and didn't even comment on her crazi-ness. I was used to Valerie and how she talked, felt, and intentionally uncensored herself. I don't ever remember her being any other way.

"All right, boy. How do I look?" She posed in some tacky-ass clothes.

I had to stuff my mouth with a forkful and a half of Alfredo to keep from laughing. "Um, Ma, why don't you ever shop at Morgan's boutique? Do you want me to call her down here so she can give you a woman's opinion?" I didn't want to tell Mom Dukes she was looking like a damn unicorn.

"Humph, I'm not stupid, boy. I know what you're trying to say. Hell, I birthed yo' black ass, so I know what you're thinking." She flipped me the finger, then turned back to the mirror. "But I don't need you or your preppy-dressing Miss Thang validating my drip. I know I look good."

"Your drip?" I fell out laughing loud as hell. "A'ight then, new school. You got it then." I wasn't even surprised that she was up on Plies.

My mom listened to all genres of music from any artist as long as she vibed with a verse or the beat. Soap operas and the radio, soap operas and the radio—that was her rotation day in and day out as she puffed on cigarettes and joints. She was the reason I had a love for music.

"So, where are you about to go anyway?"

"Bingo," she replied.

"Stop playing, Ma. You can just tell me none of my business if you don't want me to know."

She snickered. "Even though it's not your business, you're right, but I am going to bingo. I'm not playing."

"Wow, I'm in shock. Since when do you play that ol' granny-ass game?" Growing up, I only remembered her shooting dice, throwing cards around the table, and playing backgammon with her loud, gossiping-ass friends.

"Since I turned 50 years old, li'l nigga. You don't think it's time for me to slow down? I only been on the go since I came out of your cracked-out grandmother's coochie." Valerie's delivery was always raw, which was where I got my reckless mouth from.

I shook my head and laughed. We were both mean for talking about our peeps like that. "Ma, don't take this the wrong way, but I don't think you'll ever slow down. You'll be dead and in the ground but causing earthquakes."

"I shouldn't have hit you upside the head as much as I did when you were a kid. You ain't got no sense." She giggled and rolled her eyes.

"Anyway, Ma. I gotta kick it with you about yo' nephew."

"Huh? Why?"

"'Cause he off in that shit." I went into the story, which left my mom's jaw dropped.

Miranda

Today was my first day back at work, and I was stomping around all day with an attitude, ready to go home. I was also praying Amp didn't show up. I saw him calling, but I wasn't fucking with him. He was wrong as hell for letting his girl get at me at the club. Matter of fact, he didn't have to call me over to his section trying to be thirsty—having his cake and eating it too. I was cool, in my feelings or not, chasing a check on my own terms. But I already knew he was gonna bring his ass up to my job. He was the most unavailable nigga-with-terms that I'd ever known. I hated that shit got messy with us.

Even after getting home from Urgent Care, I was up with my son, cranky and going through the motions. He normally wasn't a fussy baby, so I didn't know if he was picking up on my vibes, but he cried all night—to the point where I left him in the crib and smoked a fat blunt in the shower while my tears flowed down the drain. I missed my baby daddy with my whole entire soul. Struggling would've been the last thing me and mine would've been doing.

Work was finally slowing down, and I was happy about it. It was late afternoon and about time for my lunch, and I was starving. I hadn't gotten a chance to eat breakfast because the midnight shift consisted of a bunch of lazy CNAs that didn't do shit but collect their hourly pay. I came in, changing beds, diapers, giving late meds, and even giving showers to those patients they'd left pissy all night. Sometimes I hated working this job, but I was really trying to stay out of the club to honor my baby daddy's wishes. I knew he was rolling over in his grave at how my life turned out.

"Hello, Ms. Curry. Excuse me for interrupting you, but may I have a word with you?"

I stepped off the elevator to a strange man getting up from the sitting area in the lobby and approaching me. He was dressed in slacks, a button-up shirt, and a blazer—real coplike. And then he flashed his badge and confirmed it.

"Umm, what for?" I stuttered as my nerves kicked in.

"I'd rather go somewhere more private," he requested.

I looked around while he kept his eyes locked in on me. I could feel him taking in my energy, body language, and probably what I was thinking.

"Maybe y'all can go in the break room, Randa. I won't let anyone come in there." The receptionist popped into the conversation.

"Maybe you should mind your own fucking business." I couldn't stand these nosy-ass females.

All she had to do was keep her head down and her lips zipped, but of course, they loved seeing me sweat. It didn't matter if I was in the club or not. These hoes stayed hating on me. It clicked then that ol' girl in the elevator might've got questioned about Amp and was trying to get me to dry snitch on myself. Everything started coming together 'cause the receptionist was the same one from when Amp popped up here acting all crazy.

Damn, Amp. I told you. I swallowed hard, trying to mask my worry. "Come on, Officer." I walked toward the break room with him following close behind. I was chewing my lip hard as hell, trying to balance my nerves and brace myself for whatever he was about to come at me with. I hated having to deal with the cops.

***

Two hours later, I was shaking like crazy on the gas pedal, and I damn near swerved off the road. The drive home to the comfort of my living room felt like it would never end as my phone rang off the hook. I knew Omari's mother was worried sick, but it was too hard bottling my emotions so she wouldn't hear the worry and fear pumping through my body. I was riddled with anxiety, driving in circles for the last thirty minutes, trying to make sure I wasn't being followed. I was terrified. At this point, I didn't know if my phone was tapped or if they were sitting at the house watching my moves. If my baby boy wasn't at my place, I probably would've jumped on the highway and left Detroit in my rearview. Running away from my problems and starting over in another city seemed the best plan ever if only it could be executed easily.

The air had grown so heavy in that interrogation room that I damn near choked on my own oxygen. It felt like a claustrophobic cage. Without a doubt, I know the relentless cop picked up on my uneasy body language. I kept shifting around in my chair, picking my gel manicure, and biting my bottom lip whenever the guilt of robbing these patients of actual quality of care started echoing in my conscience. Until then, I'd been turning a blind eye to how indifferent I'd been to making these old people suffer for a few extra dollars. The accusatory stares the detective shot into my soul really fucked with my mental. I'd been in and out of that conference room a hundred times with my peers, but the cold walls seemed to scream that I was guilty as they closed in. Each question the detective threw at me was like he knew each and every intricate detail of Amp's and my hustle like he was hip to Dr. Basheer's bigger scam. He kept asking why I worked so many of his cases when three other doctors were on the rotation roster, not knowing that I'd only physically laid eyes on one of those physicians. The other two relied heavily on telehealth, so they didn't have to step foot on the premises. This whole nursing home was run illegally, but they only seemed interested in Dr. Basheer and me.

At first, I was playing it dumb, like I was only doing my job, but then they dropped printouts on the table of his billing statements that had the injections I'd been administering all over them. I damn near fainted, and the truth almost slipped free from my trembling lips when they told me how many years I'd be facing for illegally giving patients shots when I didn't have a license to give shots in the first place. I wasn't certified in Michigan to do nothing but wipe shit and give sponge baths. I was so fucking scared. I had a baby to think about. With his daddy dead, he couldn't have a mother in prison. I needed to be free to raise my child. I wasn't trying to work with them, but it wasn't looking like I had a choice. They wanted me to give up Dr. Basheer, but I knew that meant I also had to give up Amp. Doc wouldn't take the fall for the entire operation, and I knew that for sure. I was in a bad situation and didn't have a clue how to get up out of it.

Chapter 23

Morgan

"Have a great rest of your day, Professor." I handed in my test, then waltzed out of the lecture hall after she nodded for me to do the same.

Unlike most of the times I took her tests, I wasn't the last one done, and I was walking out with my head held high with confidence this time. I'd taken the test. It hadn't taken me.

"Hey, what happened to you today? Why weren't you in class?" I called Bryce as soon as I got to the hallway.

"I got sick last night, and it poured over into the morning. I think it's a stomach bug," he groaned into the phone, sounding like he was about to die.

"Oh no, I'm sorry. You do sound terrible. Is there anything you need? Medicine? Soup?" I couldn't believe I was offering to go to his house, but for as much as he'd helped me this semester, I felt like it was the least I could've done.

"Aww, aren't you so sweet. As much as I'd like to see your beautiful face and think it'll make me feel better, I don't want you to catch whatever I've got just in case I'm contagious."

"Well, thanks for thinking of me. But if you change your mind and need me to drop some stuff on your porch and dash, just message me the address and wish list. As much as you've helped me, I don't mind."

"I know you don't. But you also don't owe me anything more than what you've already given."

"All right, but the offer still stands. You know I'm not good for any notes, so don't even ask for those," I laughed. "But you better get in touch with the professor so you can take the retest."

"Yeah, I'm already on top of it. I shot her an email with my Urgent Care paperwork attached. But how do you think you did?"

"Actually, Bryce, I think I did pretty well. Maybe a high B."

"Whoa! I hope you did, and with the confidence I hear in your voice, I'm sure it is. You've been busting your ass trying to up your grade, and it's working."

"I sure as hell hope so. The last thing I want to do is get to the end of the semester and fail. I don't know if I'd have the confidence even to try again."

"In my opinion, you won't even have to cross that bridge, but if you do, don't stop the race because a hurdle falls. Get up and keep running. Third place is a win. Tenth place is a win. Even the man who comes in last wins. It's the person who doesn't finish the race who loses. And you don't strike me as a loser."

"You should really think about social work or something, Bryce. You'd make a good counselor." He was always so encouraging.

"You're funny," he laughed. "But I've gotta go. I'll chat with you later." He abruptly ended the call, which was strange because I usually rushed him off the phone.

"Well, bye to you too, Bryce." I cleared my log just in case Amp wanted to play inspector with my phone, then rolled the windows down, jumped on the freeway, and headed back to the hood.

Amp

"What up, doe, partner? Are you good?"

"Yup, yup. It's a buck. Everything went smooth and is in place. Just made it back to the crib to shit and shower. Then I'll be yo' way." He gave me the rundown on how shit was shaking without saying too much. After that, we hung up.

Raj handled business. Always had. I wasn't even worried about how he was moving. It was my cousin that I wasn't trusting. I hadn't even needed Raj to tip me off to see Shylo's envy or how weird he was starting to move. From the time we were shorties, it had been nothing but love and loyalty and us looking out for each other when it came to niggas in the streets trying to test our gangster. Hell, real talk, we was even knocking li'l homies out over whose turn it was to fly high on the swing, trying out wrestling moves on them, and even humping on the same girls occasionally. So it had never been nothing for us to shout blood over bitches, family over everything, and that he was my brother from another mother, and we lived in each other's shadow. And till all this iffy shit, I would've died behind my cuzzo, but shit wasn't sitting right in my spirit with him nowadays.

I wasn't sure if it was the drugs that had Shylo acting funny or the fact that I was taking charge in this dope business, building off my money instead of tricking it off on women and drugs. His li'l habit had to be hitting his pockets hard. A coke addiction could drain a wealthy man's pockets, and we weren't wealthy. We were hood rich, and Shylo was hustling backward. I was hoping I wasn't gonna have to body my favorite family member, but death before dishonor was number one when it came to the laws of loyalty, so fuckin' over fam was fair game to get put on ice.

Me and Dex were chilling on the block. I watched my money get made while waiting for Raj to pull up on me so we could meet up with Shylo. We'd switched the game plan up hella after he hit Raj up trying to jump back on the mission. Instead of Raj making the whole drive, he met the buyer halfway, then dipped back to the D. And until I got to the bottom of Shylo's behavior, the whole operation was about to move differently.

"Yo, Amp. You know who this is easing up the block?" Dex was always on his p's and q's, peeping the surrounding. So off in my thoughts, I had to admit I wasn't even watching the block the way I should've been. This was another reason I had to handle the situation with Shylo. It was fuckin' with my head.

By the time I peeped who was in the car, she was in front of the house and looking scared as hell 'cause Dex still had his weapon showing. "Ay, she all good. You can chill." I put my arm over him so he'd fall back, then walked off the porch to meet Miranda on the curb. She was looking weird as hell. "What the hell you over here for? And why you ain't been answering your phone?"

"Because you know why. You could've kept your girl from busting me in the head with that damn bottle, and you know it."

"Yeah, whatever. That ain't got nothing to do with the money movement we on. You should've got at me. You're lucky I didn't come up there and drag yo' ass through them pissy-ass hallways for trying to play me close."

"Well, it's a good thing you didn't. The cops were up there questioning me last night."

"What the fuck? Last night? And your dumb, ditzy ass just now deciding to say something?" I yanked her out of the car and dragged her into the house.

"Yo, Dex, make sure nobody comes in." I gave him a direct order because I knew he'd for sure follow. After I got the door locked, I turned back to Miranda. "Strip," I mouthed to her. I wanted her down to her ass crack to make sure she wasn't wearing a wire.

"What are you doing this for?" She was gearing up to cry.

I threw my finger over her lips to silence her. We weren't having a conversation till I knew she wasn't trying to set me up. It was a red flag that as much as I'd been hitting her line and she'd been ignoring me, she just popped up talking some police shit.

"Now, tell me what the fuck is up, Miranda, and I bet not feel like you moving froggish, or it's a wrap," I threatened.

"I swear to you that I'm not moving froggish, Amp. I already know how this street shit works, and the last thing I want is for my son to grow up in foster care like I did. I just don't know what to do. I was pissed at you for not keeping me out of the way of your girl. That's why I wasn't answering or hitting you back up. It had nothing to do with me plotting or whatever you might be thinking. You know me better than that."

"Randa, man, say some shit I wanna hear. Tell me what happened with you and the cop." I was growing extremely impatient.

"Okay, this cop named Keidan came to the nursing home questioning me about the doctor, calling me out on not being certified and all the illegal billings. He'd done his homework and had all types of shit pulled from our records." She was shaking. "I don't know if ol' girl that worked the front desk said something or anybody else, for that matter, but I know those hoes aren't loyal to me and would give me up in a heartbeat."

"Damn. This ain't good at all. If they going after the doctor, then I know he gonna flip on my black ass. Do you know if they talked to anyone else like the pharmacies?"

"I haven't heard anything, but I bounced right afterward. I'm scared, though. I don't even wanna go in for my shift today. I'm supposed to be there at 3:00."

"Don't go. If the police are snooping and got cocky enough to pull you in for questioning, they're about to start closing in. They'll be back for the doctor or at his house, and I know for sure he's not going to take the blame. He might even do some fuck-boy shit and say me and you were forcing his hand or blackmailing him. You never know. But to play it safe, I'd pack up you and your son's stuff and get the fuck out of Dodge." I swooped the money that Dex was paying out off the table and handed it to her. "Toss your phone before you hop on the road and cop a burner a few miles outside of Michigan. Make sure I have the number so I can connect with you and keep you straight until shit dies down here."

"You think it's gonna get bad?" she questioned.

"It's gonna be what it's gonna be. Just make sure you keep your head on swivel."

"Okay." She quickly dressed, then rushed out of the house to her whip. She tried cranking it up several times, but it wouldn't start.

"Here, take my ride and go start packing. My homie is on his way. We'll pull down on you in a rental in about an hour." I tossed her my keys, then watched her coast up the street.

"Yo, Raj, man, I already need you here. There's a major problem on the floor," I alerted him as soon as he answered.

"Say less. I'm about to bend the block."

Chapter 24

Morgan

*"I got a couple of mansions,
Still, I don't have any manners.
You got a couple of ghostwriters,
But to these kids, it don't actually matter . . ."*

This was the fourth time I'd played Eminem's track "Lucky You." I fucked with him heavy, and he was one of my favorite rappers. "The Way I Am" was my personal anthem back in the day. Anyway, I was fresh out of school from taking a test I'd been busting my ass over and desperately needed a superstrong cocktail and a fire-ass blunt. I'd busted my ass all weekend hitting the books heavy studying, but over half the exam was on topics I hadn't memorized. My confidence was nonexistent, and I knew my anxiety would only worsen over the next twenty-four hours until grades were posted. My gut was telling me to pray for a miracle.

It had been a long, grueling twelve weeks of school, and for the first five weeks of it, I'd debated dropping out more than a dozen times. My professor was hella intense, and so were her assignments. I'd never experienced so much frustration from trying to keep up with the pace. If it weren't for my study partner, I probably would've been academically dismissed by now.

"You have a call from The Love of My Life." The computerized voice came through my radio's speakers and fucked up Em's flow. At times like this, I hated my Bluetooth being linked to my whip, but I smiled at the caller. It was Jayvon.

"Hey, baeee. What's good?" I hit the button on my steering wheel and answered.

"Nothing much, baby boo. Chilling on the block, waiting for Raj to pull up. Are you done with your test?"

"Yeahhh, but I don't think I passed it." I was deep in my feelings because I wasn't trying to retake the class. It was hard enough for me to get to this point, so a twelve-week setback would for sure knock all the momentum back out of me. It always seemed like there was some shit in the game to fuck up my game plan.

"Girl, quit trippin' and underestimating yourself. You know yo' ass is smart as hell and always has been." He was gassing up my ego, and it was appreciated.

"Aww, thank you, baby. I swear I appreciate you trying to make me feel better. I can't wait 'til we board the plane and get out of here this weekend." I hoped I didn't have to carry any bad news on our five-day trip to an all-inclusive resort. We'd never been on a real vacation, so I was super excited about this planned time and owed Lance big time for referring me to his travel agent.

"I'm ready to bounce too. Shit here has been hella crazy, and the drama with Shylo has got all kinds of shit fucked up around here. All I'm trying to do is parlay with a strong-ass drink in one hand and your ass cheek in another."

"That's not all we're gonna be doing, boy. I checked out all the sights and excursions they had to offer, and the agent signed us up for a few." I drifted off, telling him a long story about how my parents always traveled when I was a kid and came home with all kinds of great stories and souvenirs. "I can't wait to start making stamps on our passports together and collecting memories with you."

"As long as you've got a nigga penciled in to beat up them guts, then I'll play along with yo' wannabe Dora the Explorer ass." He chuckled, making me burst out laughing. He always had something smart to say.

"You get on my nerves, I swear. You don't never take anything serious."

"Shiittt, I beg to differ, and you know the streets can vouch. I'on muthafuckin' play about my paper, my package, and my respect."

"Okay, Scarface. Pipe down."

"I got yo' pipe down. Where are you at?"

"On my way home to take a nap. My brain hurts." I couldn't wait to curl up in bed and blow a fat one. "Was that a threat to come lie with me that I heard? I wouldn't mind getting a preview of what those strokes will be like when we touch down in Jamaica." The stress of that test had me feeling a mess, but I knew some dick would make me feel better.

"I wish I could, but I've gotta handle some business that's on the floor with Raj, plus make sure these niggas got the routine solid enough to hold the fort down while I'm gone. I was just checking to make sure you were straight."

"All right." I smacked my lips because that wasn't the answer I wanted to hear, but then checked my attitude because he was still thoughtful by calling and was actually making plans to dip for a few days. Amp didn't travel out of his element much unless you counted our quick turnaround trips to Chicago. I was shocked he didn't fight me on booking this trip, but at this point, I had every intention of dragging his ass on the plane, kicking and screaming if he tried backing out.

"All right, I almost tripped, but I got myself gathered. What do you want for dinner?"

"You don't have to cook—or clock me. I peeped that shit," he chuckled. "See if you can make us reservations to J. Alexanders or something smooth. I should be done with Raj-D in a couple of hours." Amp was giving it to me good this whole conversation, but I was used to him making plans and then canceling because his business overlapped in some way.

Instead of hinting that I was only halfway pacified by his gesture this time, I bowed out. Plus, I knew my nerves were bad from school, and I wasn't trying to take my frustration out on him when he didn't have it coming. Later though, I'd put my foot to his neck to have me wined and dined because I was now feenin' for some original jerk chicken.

"Okay, I'll text you the details. Love you."

"A'ight, love you too."

As soon as we hung up, Em came back blasting through the speakers, but this time I was annoyed, which was odd because I was just in my zone. It's like the universe was trying to tell me some shit was about to go wrong.

The curls of my weave were sweated out, and the hair was bothering my neck. "Yeah, I've gotta hurry up and get home and underneath the bed before I drive myself crazy. Every little thing is irritating me." I pulled up to a red light and shifted my car into park to swoop my hair into a ponytail. Thankfully, no one was behind me, so I didn't have to rush my movements. If I weren't taking my sweet time, I would've never laid eyes on the bullshit that made me snap.

Right before the light turned green, another car pulled up next to me with their music bumping. They were playing my song. I was getting ready to start bobbing my head and singing along . . . until I looked over and saw it was Amp's truck beside me with a bitch behind the wheel. Then my neck snapped back in shock.

"Oh, hell naw! This better be a muthafuckin' joke." I did a double take. Hitting my steering wheel, then wiping my eyes roughly, I knew damn well it wasn't a chick behind the wheel of Amp's car like my eyes were trying to lead me to believe.

After the light turned green, the car sped off. My fear was confirmed when I read the alphanumeric license plate. Either Amp's car was stolen, or he'd tossed a bitch the keys. Either way, it was about to be hell, so ya better believe I was about to find out. Quickly grabbing my phone from my lap, I scrolled to Amp's number and hit dial. While waiting for him to answer, I proceeded to make my move on the unsuspecting chick.

"What up?" he answered coolly.

"Who is this bitch driving your car?"

"What?" His reply was the customary "I'm caught up" response.

"Shit." I could hear him fumbling. "Don't do nothing crazy, Morgan. It's not what you think."

"Not what I think? I know it ain't what I thought. 'Cause what I thought is that I had a nigga who loved me and at least respected me. But what I see is otherwise. If I had my piece on me, I'd shoot the shit out ya little side piece."

"Naw, bae. It ain't even on that tip. She been working for me. Ask Nakeya. She know what's up for real . . ."

"Oh, that's what we calling it? Working for you? Okay. I'ma show you this work. And since it's obvious you and that bitch Keya been friendly behind my back for her to have a one-up on you, it's fuck her too."

My heart damn near pounded out of my chest. I couldn't believe this nigga really had tossed this chick his keys. He and I might've been going through our problems lately, but this was crossing the line. Plus, everything was coming together from the fight at the club. Nakeya definitely been an opp. I felt like I'd been surrounded by nothing but opps. Amp knew what he was doing, and the fact he was putting forth the effort to get underneath my skin had me ready to set it off. I was fuming with rage. Pushing my foot down on the gas pedal, I was about to stop ol' girl in traffic.

"You're dumb as fuck, Amp. I'm about to tear this ma'fucka up . . . and your li'l stripper bitch too. I knew I should've followed my gut instead of giving yo' dog ass more time to play with my mind. I'm 'bout to beat ol' girl into the ground, and if I kill her, that blood is on *your* hands. I ain't gon' feel shit." I coldly threw the phone down, feeling cutthroat and bitter. All I'd given up to get played had me hurt to the core. I didn't deserve this shit at all.

Ol' girl turned off the main street to a less busy one, perfect for what I had planned. Amp might've been laughing now, but I was gonna have the last chuckle. At the first stop sign we came to, I swerved around the car and then in front of it, cutting her off. We weren't in the hood yet, but about a few miles from it.

Seconds later, the horn sounded off to the point where my head started pounding even harder. She was lying on the horn with her eyes fixated on me.

She almost slammed into my passenger side but pumped the brakes on Amp's car just quick enough. When her eyes hit mine, she smirked, then leaned back in his leather seat. This broad really felt she had a one-up on me. My thought was confirmed when she threw up one of her fingers and let her smile spread wide from a smirk.

"Yup, okay then, bitch. Since you want it with me, you've got it," I said, smacking my gum.

My trusty pistol was tucked away in my purse, but I was a real hitta that always rode with more than one weapon. I hopped out of the car and grabbed the steel bat by popping the trunk. I was about to get my Babe Ruth on.

Ol' girl's eyes bulged wide like saucers when she saw me marching toward Amp's car with the bat positioned to swing. Going directly to her side, I swung it one good time.

I don't know what was louder—her screams or the sound of glass shattering. Instead of me snatching her out of the whip like I'd done Frog, I hopped up on the hood of the car. She was inside, trying to climb into the backseat.

"Bitch, I'll come through the window on ya ass if I really want to," I growled, mocking her with my swinger. Taking a deep breath, I beat the windshield like back in the day when I used to play Little League baseball. It wasn't nothing for me to knock balls out of the park better than the boys. So I was right back in my element with the Louisville slugger gripped in my hands. Blacking out for a few seconds and seeing Amp's face, I was like the Energizer Bunny trying to bash in the windshield.

The sound of his windshield cracking and spreading like the web of the deceit he'd spawned was like music to my ears. I was in the zone and about to pay this nigga back for every single time he'd made my heart shatter. The last time I swung the bat, I swung it with so much emotion that it smacked into the windshield and shattered it completely. Glass flew everywhere.

"Way to go, Morgan! You hit a home run! You should join a baseball team so you'll have a hobby," I crazily cheered myself on. Loving Amp and being loyal had slowly driven me out of my mind.

The girl screaming was what brought me back to reality. I was standing on top of the hood like I was Superwoman and had just finished killing a villain. She was terrified, and I didn't blame her. Jumping off the hood of Amp's car, I jumped back into the driver's seat of my own whip and pulled off. Instead of chasing the girl, I headed home so Amp and I could go head up.

Chapter 25

Keidan

I reviewed all our notes on the CNA and the records we'd pulled on the patients. The receptionist broke many HIPAA rules passing along the files, but that only proved the entire nursing home was operating illegally and didn't care about violations. They'd been padding their files with false information, hospital reports, and prescriptions for diagnoses the patients didn't even have. The pharmaceutical companies filling the scripts were affiliates of the family that owned the nursing home, who were all families and friends of one another. The levels ran deep.

They were scamming the system off old people left behind and forgotten about. These people weren't even getting the proper care their insurance paid for. I filed paperwork so the State could investigate and start ciphering them to nursing homes that didn't serve moldy food, smelled like dog piss, and had peeling paint everywhere—a melting pot for asbestosis and viruses. There wasn't any sense of prolonging the inevitable because it was getting shut down sooner rather than later.

I was also hoping the CNA could lead me straight to Amp. I knew she was his connect to the pills, though I didn't hint at knowing. I didn't want her giving him a one-up that the cops were investigating his organization. My informant was already a ticking time bomb.

My cell rang, and I picked up to kick it with an acquaintance for a few but quickly ended the call when my CI walked in.

"Yo, I'm here. Make it quick so I can bounce," my CI said as he entered.

"How often do I have to tell you that you don't make the rules?" I turned around to Shylo and gestured for him to have a seat.

"Man, fuck! I swear to God I never would've gotten twisted up with your dirty pig ass," he replied, begrudgingly sitting down.

We went through this damn near each time we met up. Shylo didn't walk into the station on his own to flip on his associate but was pulled over and picked up while in the act. He was en route to deliver some product to Pennsylvania, and I followed him. Before he could cross over the Michigan state line, I pulled him over and flipped his ass, then sent him on his way to deliver the product like nothing happened. I gave him one option—either go to prison and take the fall for the operation Jayvon "Amp" Banks was running, or drive way with his freedom for his full cooperation to bring down Amp. And, of course, he started singing like a bird. Shylo was how I learned about the CNA and the raggedy-ass nursing home. Even though I wasn't writing him into this case, I'd already alerted the township police department where Shylo was delivering the product so they could also start investigating the operation. I didn't owe Shylo any loyalty. My loyalty was to the law.

"Do you have anything for me, Shylo? My boss is ready to start closing in."

"Naw, I ain't got shit else. And I hope y'all go in there clean like you promised. The last thing I need is for Amp to think I had anything to do with this."

"You won't have to worry because he'll be off the streets."

"Man, you really are dumb to how street shit works, huh? It don't matter if he's behind bars. I can still get touched if y'all let shit get messy. And I'm not trying to have my street cred trashed, either. Won't nobody fuck with me if they know I've been snitching. That's a death sentence around the way."

"Look, Shylo—I will do my best and explain to my boss that you can't take the stand. I'll even put in a request for witness protection as well. But I can't make any promises."

"You better do more than make promises. You better make some guarantees."

"I know you're not threatening an officer of the law." I gritted my teeth, locking eyes with the low-level thug to remind him *I* was the head nigga in charge, no matter what quick bit of courage he might've been feeling at the moment. "Don't forget who I am and the power *I* have. I can arrest your ass right now."

He shook his head, mumbled "fuck," then dropped his head into his hands. "Keidan, man to man, all I want is for you to honor your word. I've been more than coopera-tive. I've damn near walked you to my own cousin's front door."

"You really didn't have a choice. Let's not forget. Now, quit complaining and tell me what you know about the girlfriend." I pulled out my recorder, and he fell in line.

Chapter 26

Amp

"Shit, I swear everything is closing in and falling apart!"

I hung up and waved Raj to the car so we could pull up on Morgan. My Karma was set up all the way wrong because the odds of her seeing Miranda in my vehicle was wild to none. I was praying shorty didn't flip and start working with the cops at this point because this was the second time Morgan had gotten at her like a wildcat. And this was at the worst time because Miranda was already shaken. I tried hitting her up while we were going to the intersection, but she was shooting me straight to voicemail. That wasn't a good sign.

Once we got to my truck, I was sick to my stomach. It was wrecked. Morgan did her big flex, breaking all the windows, knocking off the mirrors, and denting the doors to the point my insurance company was gonna probably total it out.

"Morgan, where in the fuck are you?" I yelled into the phone.

"Why you worried? I'm about to block your dumb ass. And if you don't beat me to the crib, I'm flushing yo' shit," she shouted into the phone and hung up.

I quickly tracked her location and saw her at Sassy & Classy.

"Raj, man, pull down at the boutique. This broad is going crazy." I finished pushing my whip out of the street, then hopped in the car to get to Morgan as soon as possible. Shit was too hot out here for us to be at war.

Morgan

Tears cascaded down my face as I was filled with anger. The pain I felt couldn't be concealed. I was tired of the disrespect and going back and forth with what I deserved from Amp. I wasn't about to spin the block on our relationship this time. It was fuck him and the years we'd invested. I had far too many more years left to live—and find a love that was consistent and without pain. I was tired of him cheating on me. And to have shorty driving his truck meant his cockiness was on a level I wasn't about to compete with.

The locksmith told me he'd be no longer than thirty minutes, which was lifesaving so I could gather all my books and the cash from the safe so I could bounce. While I waited, I changed the security codes to the alarms, removing both Keya and Jas as emergency contacts because I knew they'd be soft to Amp and give him the codes. I was checking out on the world and didn't care who suffered behind it. Sassy & Classy was about to be shut down for remodeling and regrouping anyway. I needed some time away from Amp and to be completely inaccessible to sort out my life. I sent everyone that worked for me a $2,000 bonus out of the money Amp wanted me to deposit, along with a message that we'd be closed for a week, and if they wanted to hustle elsewhere, there weren't any hard feelings.

Putting a sign in the window that said the boutique would be closed for an emergency for a few days, I shut off the lights, closed the blinds, and then left, heading home to pack a bag. I was really thinking about going on the vacation without Amp or maybe staying in Miami for the week, letting the international flight go to waste. Either way, it wasn't about to be a makeup vacay.

Getting into the car, I went to grab my phone to call Bryce. With all the madness going on, I was feening for the calmness he always brought. My being caught up in the whirlwind of bullshit in my life and wondering why Bryce kept sending me to his voicemail made it possible for the burgundy truck to go unnoticed while blocking me in. It wasn't until I looked up, seeing someone get out with a gun that I snapped out of it . . .

"Make this easy on yourself and tell me where ya nigga is at." The goon reached through the window and wrapped his hand around my hair, swiftly pulling my head toward him and pushing the pistol into my temple even more.

"Me and him are beefing. I'm not fucking with him right now to know," I disgustedly replied, hoping he'd chill . . . but no.

Whap!

He backhanded me, leading with knuckles on purpose, then pushed his pistol into my ear. My head felt like it was about to explode.

"Don't play games, bitch. I know you know where that man is at. I'm sure he don't piss without your pretty ass holding his dick."

"Damn, you sound salty like you can't get a bitch to hold *your* midget dick," I clapped back, striking a nerve because the next move he made was rocking my jaw like I was a full-blown man. I was instantly worried he'd twisted my face behind the impact because he for sure as hell temporarily blurred my vision.

"Keep running that mouth of yours, and I'm gonna shove my midget dick up in to shut you up," he threatened, muting me real quick with the clap backs. I quickly chose a different route, and that was to try reasoning.

"I told you I don't know where he's at. Probably somewhere fuckin' on the next female. That's what I caught him doing the last time we spoke. I know you think I'm lying, but I swear I'm not. Love or not, I wouldn't die behind a nigga that's not even loyal to me," I pleaded, wishing Amp would pull up and save me and set this block off. All would be forgiven. My mind started racing with ways I could get out of this shit alive, then flashed back to when Amp first took me to the range.

"You've gotta learn how to bust this bitch if I'm not around, baby." Amp wrapped my hand around the cold metal of a gun for the first time without even thinking twice.

My hands were shaking.

"Relax and breathe. Slow down. Control the moment." He stood behind me, making me match his breathing, slow and on count, till I no longer felt my nerves controlling my hands.

"Yup, that's right, baby girl. Steady, plant your feet, and tighten your chest so the kickback doesn't blow your shit back." He prepared me for my very first shot, then told me to pull the trigger.

I was about to try going for my Nina like Amp taught. Ol' boy must've noticed the desperation and intention in my eyes, though . . .

"Don't even think about it, Firecracker," he arrogantly laughed, not knowing he'd revealed his identity.

If I got out of this, he'd never live to see the day after.

"Detroit Police! Put your weapon down!"

My heart skipped a few beats hearing the police cars screeching to the scene to save my life.

"I'm not going back to jail." The weight of his gun pressing into my head had me about to piss on myself. It felt like death was staring me in the face. I closed my eyes and started praying.

Pop-pop-pop-pop!

Gunshots rang out through the air, each one echoing like a thunderclap in my ears, but not as loud as ol' boy's screams as the bullets entered his body. The weight of his body hitting the car and tumbling in on me scared me shitless and sent me into a wave of screams. I instantly slid down as far as I could in my seat, damn near underneath the steering wheel, trying to shield myself from getting shot as well. I was scared as hell.

"He's down! Phone the ambulance and the sergeant." The familiar voice blaring out orders made me frown. I went from feeling a sense of relief the shooting was over and ol' boy was disarmed to being in complete disbelief.

"Morgan! Oh my God, please tell me she's good. Weapons down!"

I hoped my mind was playing tricks on me, but when the car door opened, Bryce stood before me dressed in an all-black SWAT uniform as red-and-blue flashing lights danced behind him.

At that moment, our worlds collided.

"Are you fucking serious, Bryce? A cop? You've been undercover this entire time?" My voice cracked as reality set in. I hadn't been falling for the respectful, kind-hearted, generous man I thought Bryce was—but the enemy himself. Damn, this was what I got for moving funny. Once having butterflies in my belly over him, I now felt a rush to vomit.

"Look, Morgan, for what it's worth, I wouldn't have signed up for this task force had I known I would end up catching feelings for you. Not everything between us was work, but I have no choice but to finish what I started." His voice was filled with regret and conflict. At least I thought it was, but it was painfully apparent I'd been bamboozled for months. I was clueless about who the real Bryce was—if that was even his real name.

"Spare me any more of your bullshit-ass lies and do what you've gotta do." My response was dripping with sarcasm and rage as I stared at him with utter disgust. The only reason I didn't haul off and spit on him was because I didn't wanna get charged with assaulting his fake ass.

"Have it your way." His usually calm demeanor transformed into the cocky, overly forceful police officer's disposition I was used to. "You're being placed under arrest for drug trafficking." He yanked me out of the car by my arm and twisted it behind my back. Never ever had Bryce handled me so roughly. I didn't even know he had it in him. He'd played the timid guy role exceptionally well. "You have the right to remain silent. Anything you say can and will be held against you in a court of law." A feeling of doom came over me when I felt the cold metal cuff my wrists.

By now, traffic was coming to a grinding halt, and the pedestrians who usually walked the avenue were stuck in their tracks as if the sidewalk were quicksand. Between breaking their necks, videotaping the scene, or boldly going live on their social media to get their views up—the captured moment was embarrassing, especially when it came to my business neighbors. They'd joined in a tight bunch, exchanging puzzled glances and animated whispers, trying to piece together the events leading up to my being arrested. I was the newest tenant to their block of businesses, and after this bullshit, I was sure they'd vote to have me evicted. But right now, that was the least of my worries. I was racking my brain, trying to remember all the details of Bryce's and my conversations to see how much evidence he'd been able to gather from me. With access to my laptop, I was most worried he'd planted a bug or installed some recording device, making it a rock-solid case that not even the best criminal lawyer could get out from under.

Amp

As the handcuffs snapped shut around Morgan's wrists, my heart sank. I'd never felt as helpless as I did at that moment. I'd always known my savage lifestyle was risky, and the rebellious love I had for the streets was danger-ous, but a nigga had been too cocky to think we'd actually get caught up. For years, we'd been moving a tight ship, getting money without getting knocked, but I guess all good things really did come to an end. I was fucked up when they slid her into the backseat of the patrol car. Shorty looked broken down, like she wasn't gonna make it one hour in jail. Morgan wasn't built to be locked up. She'd already been at me hard about giving up this Bonnie and Clyde lifestyle. I knew I had to move swiftly to get her up outta there.

"Damn, you think sis gon' be good?" Raj read my mind, plus Morgan's body language.

"I hope so, at least till I get Leo on the case." I kept a criminal attorney on the payroll for moments like these, hoping there'd never be moments like these. He answered on the second ring.

"Mr. Banks, to hear from you must mean I have some work to do. What can I do for you?" He was ready to work, and that's exactly what I needed to hear.

I ran down Morgan's name and the unit taking her into custody. I also told him what Miranda said about a cop investigating the nursing home. With a few particulars, he promised to return my call in a few hours.

"Get in touch with one of the homies we got a connect with and make sure my girl ain't fucked with till we can get to her. Leo needs a few hours to catch wind of what's going on and see what's up with a bond."

Raj was on his phone just as quick to a shorty he was fucking with that was a cop. Not all people with badges were bad ones. She promised to make sure Morgan was straight as long as Raj promised to spend a few nights. I owed him big time for the barter, but getting Morgan out was a win the whole team needed.

"You might as well book us all some flights out of the country before that bougie bitch has us all behind bars," Val fussed instead of sliding on her kicks, laying low.

Raj's girl put him on alert that they were putting warrants out on all our heads and to get out of Dodge before they showed up on our doorsteps. The first person I called was Dex so he could clear the trap and get off the block before he was caught holding the bag. I tried calling Shylo, but he wasn't answering my calls. Something in my gut was telling me I needed to be worried about that nigga.

"Ma, you can chill on all that bougie bitch shit and bring ya ass. I'm not trying to hear the noise. I got too much to think about and too much on the table to lose. Them muthafuckas got addresses and are doing a roundup. Hurry up!" I yelled, feeling like my freedom was about to get snatched from underneath my feet.

Morgan

The lights flickered in the sweltering interrogation room where Officer Keidan and his partner placed me and cuffed me to a table. I was sweating bullets, and my mouth was dry, and though they were both drinking ice-cold water, they hadn't even offered me a cup of tap water from the bathroom faucet. They hadn't even offered me a chance to go to the bathroom. I was miserable and musty, which I knew were tactics to make me talk. The only thing I had to say, though, was to get me my lawyer.

"Look, Morgan, my partner has told me how intelligent you are and how bright your future is. Your shop, your degree, don't let that go to waste behind a drug dealer bound to go to jail. If we don't get him through you, we *will* get him, but then, it'll be too late to take yourself off the chopping block. We're going for life behind all the dope he's pushed into the community." Keidan's partner sat across from me, trying to play the good cop really well. She wore a sympathetic expression, and her voice was laced with empathy to make me think we were on the same side. Meanwhile, Bryce's bitch ass was on his bad cop kick—as his aura was intense, and there was heavy tension between us.

"Did your partner tell you he was trying to eat my pussy too, Officer? The fuck out of my face with your stank breath and get me my lawyer. You don't care nothing about my future, so don't play me like I'm that naive. A bitch ain't even been able to get the sweat off ya water bottle. I'm not about to be a bump in your paycheck. I'm not saying shit till I know my rights for real. I've been bamboozled on some bullshit enough." My mind was a battlefield of emotions, thoughts, and uncertainties. I needed my lawyer to sort shit out and tell me my options.

"Suit yourself, sis." She got up and took me to a cell where I was to wait for my lawyer.

That's when all the shit hit me hard—I'm talking about *real* hard. The weight of my surroundings quickly started sucking the life out of me. The metallic scent of despair hung heavy in the air, intermingled with the distant echoes of conversations from other women chatting from cell to cell. My heart raced, as this was my first brush with the harsh reality of confinement, and the walls were starting to close in hella fast. I was praying the lawyer hurried. Minutes seemed like hours. I wasn't built to weather a storm like this.

Not being about to do anything more, I lay on the narrow cot that was damn near like sleeping on the floor and cuddled up in the fetal position to calm my nerves. I tried thinking back to the night Amp and I were clinking Champagne flutes with the wealthy as a way to take my mind off the harsh reality of the life I was facing. The last things I wanted to think about were our arguments and how we'd been beefing right before I'd gotten arrested. All that shit was out the window now. Real talk, I really didn't want him to find out I'd been sneaking and creeping around with Keidan. The way he'd plotted against me was the real reason I was sitting in this dungeon. They were trying to rip my freedom away if I didn't give Amp's freedom away. Even though they had a lot of evidence of his drug involvement, it wasn't enough to put him away for longer than a few years. They were trying to have his ass digging his grave behind bars. I just couldn't give up Amp like that, but I also couldn't take all the weight of our crimes. I lay there wrestling with my conscience, trying to choose between love and loyalty, wishing this wasn't my fate. With whatever design I chose, my life would never be the same.

To be continued . . .